Triple Death

And Other Twisted Tales

Carol Fenlon

p. 86
p. 169

Published in 2016 by FeedARead.com Publishing

Copyright © Carol Fenlon.

A CIP catalogue record for this title is available from the British Library.

Books by the same author

Fiction:
Consider the Lilies (Impress Books, 2008)

Non-fiction:
Skelmersdale: A New Town in the Making: Part One, From Fantasy to First Brick (Beacon Press, 2015).

Acknowledgements

Grateful thanks are due to members of Edge Hill University's Narrative Research Group and members of Skelmersdale Writers' Group for endless close reading and feedback of the work in progress. I am also indebted to Rhona Whiteford, Jackie Webb and Elizabeth Gates for our very enjoyable lunch meetings at Liverpool's Bluecoat gallery where we give and gain support, constructive criticism and encouragement to continue with the writing we love.
Elizabeth Brown is also be thanked for her help in preparing this book for publication.

For Jake and Aimée

'The Treatment of Prisoners' was first published in *Incite*, (2000) an anthology of prose and poetry edited by Alan Corkish.

'Play With Me,' was first published in *Radgepacket 5: Tales From the Inner Cities* (2011) Byker Books.

'Re'Writing the Book' was first published online by *Holdfast* magazine (December 2015). www.holdfastmagazine.com

'Paper Money' was first published in *Radgepacket 6: Tales From the Inner Cities* (2012) Byker Books.

'You Were Made For Me' was first published online by *Near To The Knuckle* e-zine, (February, 2015). www.close2thebone.co.uk

'When Did You Last See Your Father?' was first published in *What I Remember* (2015) EBV Press.

'Ann's Test' was first published online by *Near To The Knuckle* e-zine (October 2015). www.close2thebone.co.uk

'Half-Known Things' was first published in *Radgepacket 3: Tales From the Inner Cities* (2009) Byker Books.

'Striking Shona' was first published in *Peeping Tom* No.28 (1997).

'Walker's Legend' was first published in *The Storyteller* (undated)

'He is Perfect' was first published in *For Women*, May 1996.

Contents

Triple Death.

'A body has been unearthed at a local farm by workers while they were clearing a drainage ditch. Police were called to the site early this morning after a JCB driver discovered the remains in his shovel at Blackmoss Farm near the village of Penslow in Lancashire.'

Peggy dropped the iron onto the ironing board. Her legs buckled and she sat down suddenly on the stool behind her. The air rushed out of her lungs in a puff. The pile of freshly ironed clothes tipped over and fell in a heap on the floor but Peggy didn't notice.

So it had come at last. The radio reporter droned on but she had no need to hear more. For a long time she'd waited for this to happen but these last fifteen years, since Philip died she'd let it go, it had slipped from her mind for weeks at a time. For the last few years she'd scarcely thought of it at all, it had passed into the realm of story. She was a different person now. But suddenly here it was again, as fresh as the night it had happened, just like the nightmares that had caused her to wake screaming for years, like the visions that had haunted her sleepless nights, brilliant in every detail.

She could see Lionel even now, lips drawn back tight, spittle spraying in her face. He had that vacant wild look that he always got when he was so far beside himself with rage that he barely knew what he was doing. This time he was worse than ever. She was gagging, begging, her hands clawing helplessly at her throat where he held her pinned against the kitchen wall, punching and slapping her.

'I'm going to do for you, you whore.'

Someone had told Lionel about Philip, even though they had been so careful. He'd been waiting for her when she came in from their rendezvous. She pulled at his iron fingers, blackness blurring her thoughts. Just as she was giving up, dissolving into the dark, he let go, standing over her as she slid to the floor gasping and coughing. Bitter fluid rose up from her stomach into her throat, into her nose even. When she opened her eyes he had his back to her, ramming the poker in the range. He turned, grinning at her terrified face. His eyes were devoid of anything human.

'No one will fancy you when I've finished with you.'

The thought of the poker, heating up, glowing red, coming near her face- she knew he would go for her face- blotted out all reason. Terror flooded her bowels, her bladder stinging and tingling. She got to her feet, looking for escape. He was between her and the door to the living room. The back door was locked. She could never get there and open it in time. As she watched, he pulled the poker from the fire and inspected the end. It was just beginning to turn a dull red. She tried to lunge forward but he jabbed the poker towards her, laughing as she cringed away, her eyes fixed on the hot metal.

On the shelf beside her stood an old fashioned flat iron, a great heavy thing they'd bought in the early days of their marriage as a period ornament for the farm. As he bent down to replace the poker in the coals, she seized it and brought it down as hard as she could on his head. She couldn't afford a mere glancing blow, it was him or her. Still, she was surprised when he went down with a grunt.

He lay on the rug in front of the range. She poked him with her toe and he groaned. As if everything inside her was coming to pieces she began to shake so badly that she had to hold on to the shelves at her side. She became aware of the weight of the iron in her hand and the pain in her wrist from the force of the blow. She bent to set it down on the rug, not taking her eyes off her husband. He was breathing; she could hear his breath rasping in and out of his open mouth. A trickle of blood ran from his nostril round the rim of his lip. It wasn't normal breathing but he was alive. If he got up now he would kill her.

Her wrist was too painful to lift the iron again. The shaking was slowing down now. She could see, make sense of things, think what to do. She looked round the room, then down at her shoes, unthreaded her shoelace and looped it round his neck. It almost made her sick, lifting his head to get the lace under him, but she swallowed back the bile and closed her eyes as she fumbled to make a slip knot. She kept her eyes closed and she pulled, thinking of nothing except the endless noise of his breathing. Would it never stop? At last, there was a rattle, then silence. No more torment. The house was quiet except for the clock that ticked so slowly on the wall. She took off her coat and laid it over Lionel, then went out to the hall and called Philip.

'Lionel's dead. I've killed him.'

The five minutes he took to get there seemed like forever. Lionel still lay face down on the kitchen rug.

Philip rolled him over. He groaned. Terror turned her voice to a squeak.

'He's dead, he's dead, Philip. Dead bodies do make noises, don't they?'

Philip knelt down. He put his head close to Lionel's. 'He's still breathing.'

Philip was white. He looked at the bruises already swelling her face, the necklace of purple finger marks round her throat. He got up and stroked his fingers over her face, tried to pull her into his arms.

'Don't, don't.' She stiffened If she let herself lean against him she would melt and be good for nothing. Philip pulled the poker out of the fire, looked at the vibrant red metal, raised an eyebrow at Peggy. She began to shake again.

'Bastard.' Philip laid the poker in its holder.

'We'll have to finish him off,' she found herself saying.

'He's done for anyway,' Philip said, pushing Lionel's shoulder with his foot. He looked down at the iron-shaped dent in his skull, picked up the iron and looked at the bits of hair and blood sticking to it. He took the iron to the sink and washed it while Peggy stood rigid, still holding on to the shelf unit. She had to keep watch on

Lionel, in case he moved while her back was turned, sneaked a hand out and grabbed her ankle.

Philip came back with her kitchen knife, the one she used for peeling vegetables, and a towel. It was soon over. Even the stink of blood in the room couldn't prevent the rush of triumph she felt that at last she was free of him. It sang in her blood like a choral accompaniment to the slip-slop of her loose shoe as they stripped Lionel of everything; clothes, identity, dignity. They cleaned up the mess and dragged him out of the house in her coat. She couldn't really believe it until he was safely buried in the yielding bog behind the farmhouse. She insisted on taking the spade from Philip and shovelling the last layer of wet soil over him herself. All the time they were burning her coat, Lionel's clothes, the bloody towel, she struggled between horror and laughter.

The guilty knowledge of what they had done blighted their lives, but while Philip was alive they shared it. He had made it bearable and they were still able to be happy together, and then afterwards, well she had begun to forget, like she was forgetting so many things nowadays.

The iron was hissing. She stared at it, surprised at this modern gleaming thing when she expected to see the black flat iron, sticky with Lionel's blood and hair. She stood up and switched it off. The radio was playing music now. Was it possible she had dreamt the whole thing?

Her doorbell rang. It was Josie Leadbetter from the next flat. 'Have you heard the news? They found a body, out on the moss, near your old house.'

Peggy nodded. She couldn't speak.

'We're going to have a look. Are you coming?'

Peggy shook her head.

'You look a bit peaky, dear. Shall I make you a cup of tea?'

'I'll be all right,' Peggy managed to say, 'I'll just sit down for a bit.' She went back into her lounge and sat heavily in her recliner. Josie hovered inside the front door.

'Must be a terrible shock for you. So near your old place. I wonder who it is?'

She couldn't suspect, could she? Peggy felt faint. It was such a long time since Lionel had 'left' her. There weren't many of the old ones still living in the village who might remember that she'd had a husband before Philip, but Josie was one of them.

'The cleaning lady's going to run us over there, that new one, what's her name?'

'Kristina.' Peggy whispered.

'That's right. There's me and Doris, so there's room for you too. Are you sure you won't come? Do you good to get out. Warden's always saying you should get out more.'

'No, I couldn't.' Peggy tried to sound normal, to put some strength in her voice. 'I can't bear to think about it. And my legs are playing up today.'

'All right dear, I understand. I'll come and tell you all about it when we get back.'

Peggy sat a long time staring at her blank television screen while her mind replayed the years she and Philip had spent at the farmhouse. He'd wanted them to move away, make a fresh start, but she had been terrified that someone might discover their crime. Instead they went through each day with constant reminders; the spot on the kitchen floor where Lionel had lain, the hot coals in the range where he had heated the poker, the patch at the edge of the garden where he lay unmarked and unmourned.

'The bog never gives up its secrets,' Philip used to say but it wasn't true. Lionel had waited, bided his time all these years and he'd come back, to do for her just as he had promised and now there was no Philip to protect her.

How long would it be before they identified him, before they came for her?

She heaved herself to her feet, put on her best coat and hat and crept out of the flat. The scented corridors were silent. Her feet sank into the carpet as she went to the lift. The warden was in her glass cubicle in the foyer. She looked up and smiled at Peggy. 'Decided to go with them after all?'

Peggy smiled back. She went outside, but instead of catching the bus out to the edge of the village where her old home was, she caught the number twelve, up to the top of Wheeler's Hill. Hollis Lake, once a disused quarry, now a local beauty spot, had been a favourite picnic spot for her and Philip.

There was only one other person there walking a dog round the far shore, so distant that Peggy couldn't tell if it was a man or a woman. It was too cold and dull for picnics or games, a fitting day for dreadful news. Peggy sat down on a bench and thought of other days spent at the lake while she waited for the dogwalker to disappear.

'What should I do, Philip?'

A breeze ruffled the water, whispered back at her. She couldn't wait for them to come for her. Then it would all come out, the beatings, the abuse, the shame. She couldn't bear the thought of the whole village gossiping; everyone at Rose Court, Doris, Josie, the cleaners, all inflamed with the juicy details. And they would blame Philip, his name would be sullied, Philip who had been as gentle and kind as a man could be, who had given her nothing but happiness despite the dark cloud that had always hung over them.

The dogwalker had gone. Peggy got up slowly and found a sloping edge that gave easy access to the water. She took off her shoes and hissed at the shock of cold and the soft, slimy feel of the muddy lake bed as she took the first step. The cold soaked its way up her legs, taking the usual pain away so that she felt only numbness. The lake bed dropped sharply and she floundered. She had never learned to swim, so her struggles were quickly over, her heart giving out even as she sank, her heavy coat weighing her down like a bad conscience.

'What have we here?' the pathologist surveyed the broken bits of body. 'Well preserved,' he peered closely at the head.

'Could be any age,' the student said. 'The police are looking up cases of missing persons over the last thirty years.'

'They'll need to go back further than that,' the pathologist laughed. 'Of course we'll be able to tell more after we've done the examination, but my guess is this is a case for the archaeologists. I'd say this body is over a thousand years old, probably more.'

'But it looks so fresh.' The student peered at the distorted face.

'Preservation process of the peat, no oxygen present, so no putrefaction. Look at the displacement of the features, that's pressure over centuries, not a few years.'

'How can you be so sure?'

'Well, I can't yet, carbon dating will tell the tale, but it's cumulative observation. Look at the injuries. This person didn't die a natural death. See that triangular depression in the skull? And look here, a stab wound to the neck, severing the carotid artery, then just to make sure, they strangled the poor bastard, see, there's the ligature, a leather strip I would say, buried deep in the flesh of the neck. Bodies like this turn up in bogs all over Europe. It's thought they were sacrificial victims to some earth focused religious cult. The injuries are always similar, triple death they call it.'

The Treatment of Prisoners

We are not being treated properly and I shall complain. So far as I know, we were not even at war when we were taken but there are regulations for the treatment of prisoners, agreed by 143 planets across the known solar systems. These regulations are being flouted here.

The identity of our captors remains unknown. They are large, pale creatures that I do not recognise but there are many species across the galaxy and I am no expert. If I had my computer system, I could probably identify them but Mawgan and I were taken while out swimming.

Home – how forlorn the word sounds. I wonder if I will ever see my wife and children again. Because we were taken alive, Mawgan and I are hopeful that they intend to exchange or ransom us but how long we can survive in these conditions seems doubtful.

Their world, unlike ours, appears to be gaseous. They have tried to construct a medium similar to ours, containing it and us in a tank which I must say is far too small. Although it has the right constituents in approximately the correct balance, something is wrong. It sustains us, just, but already a miasma of ill-being pervades.

Mawgan thinks it is psychological, the result of separation from friends and family, the horrendous journey here in an even smaller tank, which was sheer cruelty, and now this strange environment.

I disagree. The fluid is far too thick, it is a constant effort to push it through the gills and there is insufficient nutrient. I am perpetually hungry.

Mawgan has been taken away, presumably for examination. For the moment I am alone. This means I have more room to breathe but I am naturally anxious for his return.

It has proved impossible to communicate with these creatures. I have tried all the common and insular galactic languages, even the obscure and archaic dialects that were phased out long ago.

I suspect they are a horribly primitive species but I cling to Mawgan's idea that the creatures we have seen are a lower form of the planetary life, which perform the work tasks. It is true that such a system is still common on many planets in our universe.

It could explain why Mawgan has been taken away, to be interviewed by those of higher intelligence. I hope he reminds them of the penalty for breaking the treaty on the treatment of prisoners. I shall certainly let them know my opinion of the conditions to which we have been subjected.

Mawgan has been gone a long time now and it is difficult to keep up my spirits with no one to talk to. My worst fear is that we may be endlessly dragged and paraded about the planet as an entertainment for the inhabitants, much in the style of the travelling fairs which were so popular as a mean of education in my youth on our world, before we got to know better.

I remember, only too well, the fate of those unfortunate creatures, caged or tanked in unfamiliar and unsuitable environments, their suffering and indignity open to the view of all and sundry. Mawgan and I would not last long, but our deaths would be slow and painful.

There are movements beyond the glass. Something is happening. One of the pale creatures stands close, its fringed extremities stirring the fluid, making it harder to breathe. It is reaching out for me. My turn to be examined. At last I shall be able to lodge my complaint.

Soames spotted Sophie making an entrance in the foyer. His mouth went dry as he saw she was dressed to kill. She must be keen, he thought. He congratulated himself on inviting her here. The Universal was the hottest place in town, packed out every night since the chain opened up. She was smiling at him as she crossed the floor. If he played his cards right he might coax her into bed tonight.

'It's the latest delicacy, Mr Soames,' said the hovering waiter, 'rare but expensive.' Soames turned back to examine the gasping creature that flopped in the net held out for his inspection.

'It looks fine,' he smiled expansively, passing a generous tip to the man. 'Grilled over charcoal I think, with a mixed salad and a bottle of Chablis.'

Sophie's perfume wafted over him as she approached.

'A good choice, Sir,' murmured the waiter. 'You won't be disappointed.'

'Oh, the poor thing,' Sophie cooed, peering into the net as she took her seat opposite Soames.

'Nonsense, darling,' he said firmly, 'they don't feel a thing.' He winked at the waiter who nodded sagely in agreement.

'I think some iced champagne to start?'

Play With Me

It was Jordie found the body and it showed me something about him. We were just fooling around, running through the trees, kicking up the brown, powdery leaves, whooping in the silence while the birds held their songs. Looking back at me, Jordie tripped as he ran. I heard a thud, a scream, cut off quick as he realised.

'Shit!' he whispered.

I looked down in the dappled light under the restless trees, as he struggled to sit up, bits of leaf mould spattering his school jumper. He didn't seem so tough now. His chest heaved, but I didn't think it was from running. I could have sworn his eyes were red. He rubbed the back of his hand under his nose.

'Maybe he's not dead,' he said, eyeing the old man who lay flat on his back.

An ant crawled out of the old geezer's nose. I laughed. I made it sound hard.

'He's dead,' I said.

I looked at my hands. They were steady. I was pleased, but surprised. I could feel myself shaking inside. I kept

25

looking at the old man, checking to see if he was breathing, to see if he moved, like it was a game where he was playing dead and I had to catch him out.

He didn't breathe. His eyes stared up at the tree canopy. A dead leaf sat on his cheek. He had a strange, not-alive look that frightened me. I had never seen anybody look like that before.

I got a cramp in my belly and my legs wanted to run away but I was just stuck there, which I was glad about later, because I didn't want to look a nerd in front of Jordie.

'You're scared,' I said to him.

'Who? Me? Scared?' He laughed. It was true. Jordie was never scared, not of climbing into Mr Greaves's garden when the pit bull terrier was out, not of Lannigan, cock of the school, nor of his gang, not even of the junkies down in the city centre and certainly not of the big girls with short skirts and tits who teased and prodded us round the shopping mall on Saturday afternoons.

But I was sure he was scared now, even though he had his tough face back on.

He poked the old man with his toe and the body moved and I couldn't stop myself tensing for flight – if he disintegrated in a mass of maggots, if he leaped up screaming –

The old man just flopped with a leave-me-alone kind of shrug. His head turned a bit so he was looking sideways, halfway up a silver birch.

I moved my foot. I didn't want to do it, but I pushed my toe ever so slightly into his side. It didn't feel like anything, just like pushing a log, but softer. I drew my leg back and kicked him hard. The old man bounced. I hurt my toe.

Jordie began to laugh. He was on the other side of the old man. He kicked and the body bounced over to me. We were both laughing hard and we carried on kicking him from one to the other until we got fed up. My leg was aching.

We undressed him. You wouldn't believe the state of his underpants. Jordie held his nose and cut them off with his penknife.

He was fat and floppy, flesh pocked with bluish marks. We rolled him over and looked at the dark blotches on his back and saggy buttocks, along the backs of his thighs. We spread his cheeks and looked up his arsehole, turned him over and compared his cock with ours. He was a sorry sight really. It made me wonder what it felt like to be old. We couldn't work out why he had died.

'Maybe he had something catching,' I said, suddenly thinking of AIDS. I wiped my hands on his raggedy old coat. It was the same colour as the weathered tree trunks.

'Nah,' said Jordie, 'He don't look sick enough. Cold most likely, or maybe a heart attack.' He thumped the old man's chest. 'He's been here a bit. The rigor mortis has gone off.'

He lifted a floppy leg and dropped it again. I giggled. I found a stick on the floor and jammed it in the old guy's mouth.

'Cigar sir?' I said, polite as I could. He had a grizzly old beard and moustache and a mouthful of rotten old teeth. One or two broke off when I shoved the stick in. Jordie laughed and laughed. I felt clever. I was usually the butt of the joke. It felt good to be dishing it out to someone else.

Jordie opened his penknife.

'Haircut sir?' He began to slice off the few shreds of hair the old man had stuck round his head. The grey strands fell on me and I brushed them off with disgust. We laughed till we cried.

We searched his pockets but he had nothing. A filthy old snotrag and a baccy tin full of other people's stinking dog ends. A packet of fag papers and a few loose matches and a woman's purse with 6p in it. On the ground near his feet we found a greasy old bag with a spoon, an empty pop bottle, more rags and a tattered nudie mag. That was it.

Shadows fell on us and the sun glittered low through the trees. We hadn't noticed the time passing.

'Suppose we'd better tell someone,' I said as we lay in the dead leaves, the nudie book abandoned by our feet. It was getting colder.

'We can't,' said Jordie. 'We've messed him up too much now. We'll get done.'

I looked at the body. He was right. We were always in trouble anyway. It used to be just me, till Jordie came to live by us. Even the other kids always had a go at me. I had no-name trainers and hardly ever got new clothes. Now Jordie was my friend, although even he could turn on me at times. At least no one else picked on me while he was around.

'What shall we do then? Someone else will find him.'

'We'll just cover him up with branches and stuff. We can come back tomorrow and bury him proper. He's just an old tramp. No one's going to be looking for him.'

'That'll be ace!' I was excited. I'd never buried anyone before, except a white rabbit I had when my dad used to live with us. I punched Jordie on the arm.

'Defo coming back tomorrow?' It had been a great day, best day for ages.

"Course.' Jordie punched me back. 'Sag school tomorrow and meet me by the stile over the footpath. I'll bring me dad's spade.'

'Cool.' I looked at the lengthening shadows. 'We'd better get home. I'll be late for me tea.'

'Your mam won't notice,' said Jordie and I felt like smacking him but there was no point. Everyone knew about my mam and there was no use trying to pretend any different. There probably wouldn't be any tea. I turned away and began collecting fallen branches.

Next day, I thought I would never get out. Mam had a fight with Stevie, her Cockney boyfriend and she took it out on me. She was still drunk from the night before and I had to go and get her cigs and make her eat some toast and get some coffee down before I could get out and even then she went on and on, then she cried and cuddled me and that was even worse.

It was only when I said Mr Thorne, the school head, was going to expel me if I missed school again, that she let me go. I knew there was still half a bottle of gin in her bedroom and she'd soon be flat out on it, so she wouldn't be checking up on me.

It was half-past nine by the time I got off the estate and on to the path down the side of the field that led to the woods. It was that nice quiet time when all the kids are in school and all their mums are at the shops or jangling in each other's kitchens.

I practised walking tough, the way Lannigan walked. The sun already burned my back and I smiled, thinking of the long summer holidays coming up and the fun I would have with Jordie, if I could keep out of me mam's way, that was.

I screwed up my eyes at the black mark in the distance that I knew was Jordie waiting by the stile. My heart jumped when I got closer and saw him leaning on the spade. It had rained in the night, but in the woods the ground was soft and barely damp.

It took us ages to find him. We hadn't thought to lay a trail and in the middle, all the trees looked the same but in the end we found the heap of leaves and branches. I could see one of his eyes staring through a gap in the twigs.

'This is cool,' I said, testing the ground with the toe of my trainer, looking for a nice, easy place to dig.

The next day Jordie disappeared. I knew he was going to court, for nicking stuff from the back of 'The Happy Haddock', our local chippy, but I didn't expect him not to come back.

I hung around by the woods all day, waiting for him and around four o'clock, when I could see kids coming along the footpath on their way home from school, I went round to his house, but his older brother opened the door.

'What do you want, yer little toe rag?' He glared at me. I could tell he had only just got up. He smelled like someone who had slept in their own farts all day.

'He got locked up,' he sneered, pushing his face closer to me, 'an' good riddance too.' He was smoking a rollup and he jabbed it at me.

'Now push off you scumbag and don't come round here no more.' He slammed the door on me before I could say anything and when I turned round, Helen

Rimmer and Katie Forshaw were standing across the street, watching and giggling.

I gave them a dirty look and went off as dignified as I could. Sometimes when Helen Rimmer was on her own, she would talk to me. She could be quite nice and I fancied her rotten, but I knew it was no use today, not when she had her mate with her. I was the lowest of the low in our class and she wouldn't want to be laughed at.

I went home then because it was going dark and there wasn't anywhere else left to go. I could hear them fighting even before I got to the back door.

'He's a little barstid.' Stevie was shouting in that London accent that I hated so much. 'He wants a fuckin' good hiding.'

'Well, you won't be givin' it 'im. If anyone's gonnna give my lad a fuckin' hiding, it'll be me.'

She was drunk. I stood behind the back door, face pressed up against the wood. I thought they must be in the front room.

'Anyway, he's not so bad.' Mam's voice turned maudlin. 'They've got a down on 'im in that school.'

So that was it. The school inspector had been round again.

''E's just a barstid, ' Stevie growled, anger turning sullen. ''E wants it knockin' out of 'im.'

It was no use going in. I turned around and sneaked away. I went off back towards the woods. Yesterday had been such fun. Now everything had gone wrong. The path to the woods was lonely and empty. All the other kids would be indoors now, eating beans and chips, watching TV, playing video games. I looked up at the gathering shadows, remembering Jordie waiting by the stile. I needed someone to talk to.

It was a bit scary in the woods but everything was quiet and peaceful. No one was going to get me. I stumbled about for ages, looking for the spot, although I was more familiar with the landmarks than the time before.

In the end I tripped over Jordie's dad's spade. We'd left it under some leaves, marking the place where we'd buried the tramp. I lay in the cold, damp leaves, thinking about the tramp, lying in the dark soil beneath me. He must be lonely. I wished Jordie hadn't gone away.

The woods were full of rustles and waving branches that moved on a backdrop of silence, waiting to see what I would do next.

I cried for a bit. It was okay, because no one else was there.

'What'sssssss the matter?' whispered the leaves, or was it the tramp, pushing words up through the loose soil?

'I've got no one to play with.' I whispered back and looked round quick, just in case someone was there, whispering and playing a trick on me.

'No one, no one,' whispered the trees and waved carelessly above my head.

'I'll play with you,' said the tramp and I heard him quite clear, just like he was in my head.

He must be alive, I thought, but I knew he couldn't be. I scrabbled loose earth away for a bit, where I thought his head was and then I got the spade and dug around for a bit, careful so I wouldn't hurt him. Even so, when I did find him and scraped the earth away, the spade had chopped into his cheek, like when you cut through a potato.

I cleaned the earth away from his face. It was quite dark, but I could still see he was pretty grubby, so I got a bit of tissue out of my pocket and wiped his face a bit. His flesh felt soft, like my fingers might go right through it, so I had to be careful.

His eyes were shut so I opened them, just while I was talking to him and I told him all about how horrible everyone was to me at school and how awful it was at home since Stevie came to live there.

He looked at me all the time like he was really listening and he didn't laugh or anything.

I felt better after that. I covered him up again. He was beginning to smell a bit.

'Come and play with me tomorrow,' he whispered and I thought that things wouldn't be so bad after all. When I got home I sneaked in real careful, but me mam and Stevie had gone to the club and when they came back they'd forgotten all about me.

I didn't go back to school. I went and played with the tramp every day instead. I called him Albie. I don't know why but the name just seemed to suit him. Stevie shouted at me a few times and tried to leather me with his belt, but Mam kept him off me and I stayed out of the way most of the time.

After a while, Albie started to smell really bad. He'd gone a funny colour and he looked like he was going to melt.

I was going there one morning, just about the time all the kids would be in assembly. I had to go out early so it looked like I was going to school, then I hung round till all the other kids had gone. Some of them would chase me and beat me up now that Jordie was gone.

I was surprised to see Helen Rimmer going up the footpath by the side of the field. She was on her own and she stopped when she saw me and sort of half- smiled at me.

'Where have you been?' she said. 'You haven't been to school for ages.'

Her blonde hair was tied back in a ponytail. It looked soft, straight and silky.

'She's pretty,' I heard Albie say and I jumped and looked round, but nobody was there.

'I hate school,' I said, kicking a stone. 'I'm never going back there.'

'You'll have to go in the end. They'll make you. Want a sweet?' She gave me a mint.

'Thanks,' I was surprised. 'How come you're not in school either?'

'I'm just going now. I had to go to the dentist's for a check up. Don't people stop you, you know, walking round all day in your uniform?'

I was conscious of my limp, grubby clothes. Her school blouse was fresh and crisp. I could see the outline of a lacy white bra underneath it.

'I don't hang around here. I go in the woods all day.'

'It's creepy in there.' Helen shivered. 'What do you do all day? It must be dead boring.'

'It's sound,' I said and before I could stop myself. 'There's a dead body in there. Some old tramp.'

'Yeah, I bet!' Helen turned away.

'Honest,' I said. 'Me and Jordie found him. I'll show you if you like.'

I didn't think she'd come but she turned back and followed me.

'You better not be lying, Wilson,' she said.

We went across the field. I was telling her all about the tramp, how we found him that day, but I didn't tell her everything, just about how we buried him because we were too scared to tell anyone, and all the time I felt like I was dreaming, like it was too good to be true, having Helen Rimmer out with me, just like a mate. Maybe I could even pretend to myself she was my girlfriend, but at the same time I was scared. Helen was a goody-goody. What if she told on me, told someone else about Albie? I would get done.

It was too late anyway. We were in the clearing.

I picked up the spade. I didn't even need to think now where he was.

'Is he – it, under there?' Helen seemed fascinated. She didn't seem scared, even though people were always telling kids not to go in the woods on their own.

I suppose she thought she wasn't on her own, she was with me and I don't suppose she was scared of me, the scum of the earth.

'She wants to play with you,' Albie spoke up. 'She wants you to play with her titties.'

I looked down at the ground. Surely she must have heard him.

'Come on, what are you waiting for?' he said impatiently.

It was a tempting idea. I could have Helen Rimmer here to play with me every day, whenever I wanted, just like Albie.

'Go on, go on!' He was hissing gleefully.

I tightened my grip on the handle and began to lift the spade.

Suddenly something crashed through the trees.

'I got you, you dirty little barstid!' Stevie burst into the clearing, red-faced and sweating. 'I follered you, you little git! So this is what you get up to, sniffin' round like a dog after a fuckin' bitch – an' as for you –'

He turned on Helen and her eyes rolled like a frightened deer, then she wheeled and ran and as she disappeared, I swung the spade and bashed Stevie hard on the back of the head.

It was a long time before I went home. Stevie was fat and heavy and I was on my own this time. It took me ages to dig a big enough hole and I got my own back on him for all the bad times before I finally dragged him into it. We played lots of games, Stevie and me, and he didn't call me any names at all. He wasn't my best choice of playmate, but he was better than no one at all.

'What about me?' said Albie as I walked home. 'I'll never leave you.'

'But you can't play any more,' I said crossly, remembering the awful smell the last time we had had a game.

I realised how mucky I had got during my games with Stevie and I hoped me mam wouldn't be about when I got home, so I could clean myself up without her noticing.

'She's a right barstid, anyway,' said a voice in my head and I began to laugh.

Here Lies Fred

Jack stared at the skull sitting on the end of his spade. The golden morning still shone round him, the birds went on singing but his anticipation of digging the first patch in his very own garden instantly evaporated. The fresh smell of turned earth had taken on a distinct stink of decay.

All their dreams had come true when they'd got this house. After years of scrimping, doing without, he and Rosa living in cramped, drab, damp furnished flats, suddenly – the great job, fantastic wages – and the house. It was as if they were on a roll at last, nothing could go wrong – and now this.

The initial shock however, had begun to wear off and he was already calculating the likely results of his discovery. Rosa would have a fit. She was horribly superstitious, wouldn't step on a crack or walk under a ladder. There was no way she would be persuaded to stay here now a corpse had turned up in the garden. Jack kept looking at the skull, hoping he was mistaken, willing it to turn into a rotten pumpkin or some kids long-lost football but there was no getting away from it, it was a human skull and there were more bones poking out from the hole he had dug. It was a real skeleton not a plastic Halloween jobby some joker had buried there. Suddenly he felt sick. Someone had died here and someone had buried him or was it a her? He shivered in the sunshine and looked round the bushes that hedged the neat little plot as if the person responsible might still be hiding there.

It was such a nice day and they had everything planned; Jack would dig out a new flower bed in the morning while Rosa was doing her half-day in the charity shop. When she got home they would go to the local garden centre and pick out some spring bulbs, daffodils and tulips, maybe some crocuses, have lunch in the garden centre's coffee shop and plant the bulbs together when they returned. The evening would be spent together over a bottle of wine. Jack had planned to cook for Rosa, beef bourguignon, her favourite. Now, what would happen? For a moment, he considered shoving the skull and the bones back into the hole and covering them up again but he knew he would never be able to live with himself if he did that.

There was nothing else for it, the police would have to be informed. It was only when they had arrived, with their SOCO officers in white paper suits and the police surgeon enthusiastically poking about and blue scenes of crime tape all round the house and garden, that Jack began to think of the person to whom the skull had belonged, to feel sad about his or her sorry end and to wonder what had happened.

He phoned Rosa, although he dreaded telling her. It would have been worse to let her come home as usual and walk into the pandemonium of police that filled their home. She didn't believe him at first and he had to go over it several times before she agreed to leave her job and come back. By now, he really wanted to have her beside him. He was sure the police suspected him of being responsible for the body; he'd been practically confined to the kitchen by a watchful constable, even though it was obvious to anyone that the bones were really old and couldn't have anything to do with him.

'We've only been here six weeks,' he kept telling the constable, who seemed quite happy to listen while Jack supplied him and his colleagues with endless cups of tea.

When Rosa arrived breathless from her journey, as he'd expected, she was torn between horror and morbid fascination.

'We can't possibly stay here,' was her first exclamation. 'I couldn't bear to sit out in the garden with the thought of it lying there, God knows for how long. I don't care if it's a thousand years old.' She looked at the constable. 'You don't think we had anything to do with it?'

Her cheeks were flushed and her eyes hot with excitement. She looked particularly attractive, if the constable hadn't been there…

'We're contacting the previous owner,' the policeman looked pointedly into his empty mug.

'He's a doctor – Dr Sandhar,' Jack said. 'That's all we know. We never met him.' The house had been vacant when they bought it; everything had been done through solicitors.

The police surgeon came in through the open kitchen door. He might have knocked, Jack thought resentfully.

'May I wash my hands?' he at least had the manners to ask. He was smiling happily, more as if someone had just told him a great joke rather than presenting him with unidentified grisly remains to examine. Rosa looked on in horror as he scrubbed up at her kitchen sink. Jack thought she would probably want to throw out all the china that had been drying on the draining board.

'Well, I think we've solved this little mystery,' the surgeon went on, drying his hands on the kitchen tea towel, which Rosa took and promptly deposited in the kitchen waste bin. 'Any chance of a cup of tea?'

Jack put the kettle on. He glared at the surgeon. The man looked extraordinarily cheerful for someone who spent his time examining dead bodies. And there wasn't anything to be cheerful about. What would happen to the value of their property once it got out there'd been a body in the garden?

'Nothing to worry about, Sir,' the surgeon said. 'Nothing at all – it's not a body – well it is, but not in the usual sense.'

Jack stared. So did Rosa and the constable.

'It's a medical skeleton. If you'd looked closely you'd have seen the wires holding it together. Mind you some of them had come away, that's how the skull ended up on your spade. Been there a good few years.'

Rosa gasped, then began to giggle.

'I didn't look that closely,' Jack said, feeling his face turn red. 'It was a bit of a shock.'

'They don't use them any more. We all had to have them in my day, when we were training. You know we had to pay for them ourselves. Bloody expensive on a student grant. Imported from India; of course it wouldn't do nowadays.'

'What'll happen to it – her?' Rosa sat down at the table.

'Oh, it's a male. Well, that's up to you, isn't it? I suppose you could keep him if you wanted to, or maybe you'd rather we disposed of it?'

'I should jolly well think so,' said Rosa, accepting a cup of tea from Jack. 'What would we want with such a thing?'

'I don't know,' Jack said after the surgeon had gone and the constable had disappeared outside to assist with the clearing up. 'It might have been quite nice to keep him, we could have made him a resting place under a rose bush or maybe a tree, with a headstone – 'Here lies Fred – a long way from home.'

Rosa wasn't impressed and threw the clean tea towel at him. Jack, remembering her hot eyes and flushed cheeks was about to chase her round the kitchen table when the constable returned to tell him he would have to come down to the station to make a statement and to sign over the property for disposal.

Jack was still chuckling over his unwanted property as he prepared to leave the station later that evening. As he waited for the desk sergeant to let him out, he was accosted by a large Indian woman in the foyer.

'I believe you bought my house? I'm so sorry for causing you such trouble. That old skeleton lying around full of dust for so many years. How to dispose of it? I couldn't think of anything else but to bury it, and then of course, I forgot all about it.'

'It's all right,' Jack said. 'It gave me a turn when I dug it up but I'm just glad it was a false alarm.' He didn't like the way the woman was looking at him, there was something shifty about her; she was smiling too sweetly. Her eyes were calculating, despite the smile, watching him – for what?

'Your husband isn't with you?' He looked round wishing someone would come to rescue him.

'My husband?'

'Dr Sandhar. It was his skeleton, right?'

Her smile turned to a tigerish grin. 'What makes you think that? I am Dr Sandhar. My husband died many years ago.'

At that moment the desk sergeant returned. 'Thanks for coming down so promptly to clear this up,' he said to the doctor.

'No problem,' she smiled at Jack again as the sergeant released the doorlock to let her out.

'All's well that ends well,' the sergeant remarked to Jack as he left.

Jack stood on the station steps, watching Dr Sandhar get into a large Audi parked in the station car park, the memory of her smile lingering like the Cheshire cat's grin. If what he suspected was true, it was a fiendishly clever way of disposing of a murder victim. He began to shiver. 'No, it couldn't be,' he said to himself as he walked away.

Re-writing the Book

The dark figure scurried, black robe dragging in the dry leaves blowing round the spiral stone steps; steps that were worn to the tread of centuries past.

Musty air parted, laden with dust and smells of powdered bones; dry death; things once rotten, now light and brittle. Cobwebs snagged unnoticed on the shoulders, mingling grey threads with darker stains of age.

The figure hurried on, its stunted arms ending in huge hands that clutched and pulled on the dry-stone walls. Upward, upward and out under a black sky that moved and swirled, announcing a coming storm. No sun or moon, just lowering darkness, suddenly riven by lightning, throwing into relief the worn turrets, the squat figure turning, the black hood pointing backwards, turning to show the front, face hidden in cowled shadows, the face –

Allie bolted upright. Her chest heaved. She stared at the blank bedroom wall, still seeing the turrets, the shadowed hood.

Her gasps slowed and she moaned with relief as she realised where she was, realised it was only the dream – again.

Rick turned uneasily. His eyelids fluttered. Allie laid her hand on his warm shoulder, re-assuring herself. Her other hand felt her head, her hair sticking down, soaked with sweat. Sweat ran across her eyebrow and down her cheek. She shivered and pressed her fingers tighter, holding on to Rick.

'For Christ's sake, Allie, not again,' Rick muttered, waking and pulling away from her.

'I'm sorry, I'm sorry,' she gasped, breathing easier now. Hold me, she willed, just hold me, but he sat up and switched on the bedside light, the lines of his body tense and angry.

'Look at the time. Quarter to three. Allie, you know I have to be up at six.'

'Rick, I can't help it.' She felt tears coming, pushed them back.

'We can't go on like this,' Rick turned off the light and flopped down. 'Either you'll have to go and see someone about these dreams, or I'll have to move into the spare room.' He turned his back, pulled the sheet tight across his body.

Allie lay down, silent so he could sleep. Separate rooms. The idea threatened her. She lay stiff, afraid of disturbing Rick, afraid to sleep.

Ethundrel sat at the top of the tower, watching. The sky formed and re-formed, grey and black above him. Below, the mist swirled, punctuated by the tops of stunted trees. Except for the whisper of wind through the castellations, it was quiet. He hugged his rusty robe about his knees, watching for movement. Something was wrong, something was happening inside his head. His eyes fixed, staring into the distance, into a sky that was blue, not black.

One corner of his mind wondered that there was no pain from that sky, but the rest was filled with amazement at the creature that walked there; a female with small eyes, blue as the cloudless sky, her hair pale yellow and silky, like the tassels on the barley that he nursed and coaxed each year. Grass grew in abundance and red flowers were visited by insects that buzzed in the scented air.

Ethundrel could see drops of dew glittering in the joints of leaves and tracing the edges of petals, despite the shining sun, but the woman seemed oblivious to the wonder of this. She walked aimlessly and a frown marred her face.

The buzzing changed, grew louder, intolerable. Ethundrel put his hands to his ears, transfixed. A monster came flying at him, black and shiny, with glaring eyes, roaring, so fast that he could not move aside and the woman still seemed unaware.

He screamed to her, hands outstretched to ward it off, and fell back, striking his spine against the stone turrets, clutching to stop himself tumbling over into the misted tree tops.

His eyes hurt, stabbed by the rays of sun that had pierced the rolling blackness while he had been looking at that other sky, and he threw up an arm to deflect the light, quickly pulled over his hood and rubbed away the stinging pain beneath his eyelids in the cool darkness afforded by the cowl.

His breath came ragged as he lay back on the floor, reducing the fearful monster to the dream image it surely was, but a screw of longing turned inside him, remembering the impossible green of the grass and the silken beauty of the woman's hair.

The burning sky had not seemed to touch her. Ethundrel got to his feet. The rolling cloud had once more put out the beams of light. He climbed down into the dim cool of the tower, the echoing steps familiar under his feet.

By two a.m. the party had wound down to the quiet intimacy that Allie liked best.

She looked at Rick, who was chatting to Alan across the room. He leaned against the wall, over Alan, his face animated. His brown hair flopped forward into his eyes. She wanted to stand behind him, run her hands over his chest, press herself close and feel his back and buttocks.

'How often do you have this dream?' Maria's large, dark eyes were fixed on her.

Allie bit her lip, brought back to the coterie of women. At least Maria was taking it seriously. She shrugged.

'Two or three times a week, over the last month or so.' She looked into Maria's eyes, saw sympathy, wobbled on the edge of tears and looked away, at Rick.

Patsy lit a joint and sucked on it. Her straight blonde hair swung across her face as she shook out the match.

'Is it always the same?' She leaned back, holding her breath, then puffed out the smoke.

Allie took the joint, steadying herself. She hesitated, guilt touching her lightly, but the promise of pleasure, release from her fears, overcame it. It wouldn't do any harm, she told herself, after all, she wasn't even sure yet. She took a long pull and felt better, gathering her thoughts as the smoke burned her lungs.

'More or less,' she said on her exhaled breath, passing the joint over to Maria. 'It – he sits on top of the tower. He doesn't seem to see me, or do anything, but there's a sense of awareness…' she broke off and felt in her mind, 'as if, as if each time, he comes closer to me, our worlds come nearer. I don't know – it's like each time I know a bit more about him, even though he scares me to death. Last night I saw his eyes for the first time. They were huge, but not as frightening as I thought they would be, you know, when I could only see his hood. Big blind eyes, like some night creature.'

'How horrible.' Patsy stared at her. 'What a nightmare. I would die! I would just die! Is he really scary?'

'It's not like that.' Allie almost smiled at Patsy's horror. 'It's not so much him, he's weird all right, his arms and legs don't look right, but like some strange animal there's a softness, a sadness about him. It's the place, the atmosphere, it's so black, always black – and it's somehow so – real.'

Patsy's eyes were glazed, her lips parted as she listened. Allie shook herself, smiled wryly at Maria.

'This is silly. Let's talk about something else.'

'Have you spoken to anyone else about this?' Maria sucked on the joint and passed it on. Allie picked at her skirt.

'Rick thinks I should see a psychiatrist. He thinks I'm crazy.' The words came out tinny with fear. She looked up defiantly. Maria's eyes were calm.

'I don't think that's a good idea,' she said. 'I've got a friend who's experienced in the paranormal.'

'What, ghosts and all that?' Patsy's eyes were brilliant. She leaned forward staring at Maria.

'You don't think it's a ghost?' Allie said uncertainly.

Maria shrugged. 'What do you think it is?' The joint came to Allie again but she refused it and passed it to Patsy, avoiding Maria's gaze.

'Whatever it is, it's persistent,' said Maria. 'Have you been anywhere like the tower recently, old castles, stately homes?'

Allie shook her head, puzzled. She felt cold, thinking about it. The sound of Rick and Alan laughing made her feel better.

'It's probably just some bogey from childhood, working its way out,' she said, unconsciously siding with Rick.

'Look, don't get tied up with psychiatrists. You'll end up on medication you don't need, with syndromes you never heard of. Jesus, Allie, you could end up worse than when you started. Give my friend a try. There could be all sorts of explanations for this kind of thing.' Maria wrote down a name and address on a scrap of paper.

Allie took the note, surprised. She had only spoken about the dream as a conversation opener, but Maria seemed really concerned. She realised how worried she had been herself. She had needed to talk about it. No one had scoffed. She looked down at the address. Maybe it wouldn't hurt to try it.

Ethundrel had only to close his eyes now to see the woman, but he was torn between his longing for her and the sweet things of her world, and his fear of the roaring monsters that seemed to roam her environment at will.

He sat in the cool darkness at the base of a tree. The forest trees retained enough leaves to protect him should the sun come out. Hunger had driven him from the tower, searching for movement, life. He had caught a rabbit, a sickly specimen, but meat of any kind was rare.

The woman was talking among other women in a room. They drank from clear vessels. There were no monsters. Her beauty shone against the other two.

''Tis not a dream,' Ethundrel whispered to himself, conscious of his wakefulness. A vision? But why? He pondered as he made his way back to the tower through the silent wood, the rabbit swinging from his waist.

'There are two ways of looking at this.' Portia Vane tented her fingers, grey eyes regarding Allie calmly. 'Either you're trying to tell yourself something, or someone else is.'

'What do you mean?' Allie was taken aback. 'You mean my subconscious?'

'Subconscious – unconscious, whatever. Maybe.'

'I thought of that,' said Allie, 'but what? And why the hooded figure?'

'Something hidden, somebody tall and threatening. Some family secret?' Portia smiled.

'But I come from a happy family. Really,' Allie cried. 'And why now, suddenly now?'

'Has something changed recently? Something different in your life?'

Allie felt uneasy. She began to feel resentful of Portia's line of questioning. What qualifications did she have for all this analysis? Only the questionable validity of Maria's recommendation.

She looked over the sparsely furnished room. There was nothing to give any clues regarding the owner's experience of the paranormal. No crystal balls, pentacles, no framed certificates on the walls, and yet – perhaps she was right. Allie's hand covered her stomach.

'I hadn't thought of that,' she said haltingly.

Portia raised an eyebrow but didn't press her.

'Look, I'm no psychiatrist,' she said, 'I've just talked to a lot of people who have had paranormal experiences. Call it a hobby, an interest. Maybe I'll write a book about it one day. Anyway, repeated dreams of this kind of intensity indicate some kind of message is trying to come through, if not from inside, then from out.'

'You mean a ghost?' Allie sat back in her seat.

'I don't like labels,' said Portia, sitting back too. 'It could be something as simple as vibrations, trapped in a building you've visited. Something that happened in the past, never resolved, forever sending out vibrations. You may be sensitive to it, pass by and pick it up. Might have nothing to do with you personally.'

Allie stared.

'On the other hand, it might.' Portia tapped a long red fingernail against her teeth. The room seemed darker, almost menacing despite its simple furnishings. Allie suddenly felt afraid. The very ordinary Portia seemed threatening. She wanted to escape.

'Well, what should I do?'

'Try to listen dear, that's my advice.' Portia smiled encouragingly. 'If it's trapped energy, it will dissipate through you after a while. If it's important it will come out anyway. Just try to relax. Don't fight it. It doesn't mean you any harm.'

Allie thought about it as she drove home. How could she relax when she was so terrified of the dream? Each night she fought sleep, tense with fear. She was still biting her lip when she let herself into the flat.

Rick was home and in a good mood. She didn't tell him about Portia Vane. He would scoff and get annoyed that she hadn't followed his advice. Anyway, she had other news. She shrugged off her uneasiness and put the dream memories firmly to the back of her mind.

She sat at the dining table as Rick drained a pan of pasta. Her hands stroked her stomach under the table as he served the meal.

'I've got something to tell you,' she said. gently. 'I went to the doctor's today.'

Ethundrel left his room in the tower and went slowly down the turning steps. He hesitated at the bottom, outside the door on his left opposite the arch that led outside. He pushed the unlocked door and showers of dust flew as it creaked open. He had never opened the door since Caladriel had died.

He stopped in the doorway, mind rolling back to the time when there had been others. His mother, Caladriel his little sister and the one-legged man. He struggled for the name. Cordor? Was it Cordor?

Even then they had mostly kept out of the main building. It had made them afraid. Cordor had remembered the men who had lived there, men who worshipped the god and wore long skirts. The god had caused their deaths, all the deaths. Cordor had told him this as they sat round the tiny fire in the tower room on cold nights. Cordor had tried to explain it to him but Ethundrel had never understood.

His feet sank in the thick dust of the dim room. He looked up at the high carved and vaulted roof, keeping a hand over his eyes to ward off the coloured light that filtered through the stained glass windows.

They had kept his mother here for many days when the thick snow had come and they had been unable to dig a grave. Cordor himself had lain here waiting while he and Caladriel had struggled to make a big enough hole.

He tried not to look at the big cross but his gaze was drawn to the dull, tarnished metal. Once, when Caladriel awaited her burial, the light had struck it so fiercely it had burned his eyes. He drew closer to it, dragging his feet reluctantly. The soft rags tied round his ankles swished across the floor. Why he was there, he did not know but something had drawn him. He felt as if something were about to be explained and despite his fear, curiosity drove him on.

On the great table before the cross were candlesticks and books in woolly dust jackets. Cordor had forbidden them all to touch them. He'd said they were a source of evil. Convinced of the truth of Cordor's words, Ethundrel had put them out of his mind but now he was tempted to examine them for himself. His shaking fingers brushed dust from the largest book. The huge room seemed to hold its breath as he turned the cover, felt the stiff board, heard the seductive whisper of the first page, worn thin with age.

A rat ran across the table and Ethundrel was almost drawn away by this sudden, unexpected promise of food, but it was gone almost at once and he looked down on the strange marks on the paper, marks that meant nothing.

Page after page revealed nothing but regular rows of dots and lines. No evil came to strike him, nor explanations to account for the visions. He looked up, weary of the empty pages. All was dim and silent. He sighed, closed the great book and idly took up another smaller one and opened it to see the roaring monster from his dreams. His breath rushed out in a surprised gasp that rustled and echoed round the carved corners like a confirmatory whisper. It was a sign.

He clutched at the pages, careless of their fragility, looking greedily at the pictures; other people, dressed strangely, but people like himself, male and female, and many, many roaring monsters, not roaring now, but he had heard them in the dream.

He looked away into his mind and when he looked back at the page she was there, the woman of the dream. He bent close, huge eyes peering at the faint images. It was her, he was sure, but she was older, much older. She sat with others on a platform behind a man, a young man, clear of eye and fair of brow – and he looked so much like her.

Ethundrel's finger moved from the man's face to her face. She looked so proud. She gazed adoringly at the man who was not looking at her but out, out at Ethundrel with an air of great knowledge. Ethundrel immediately remembered how his mother had used to stroke his hair back, long ago. She used to whisper words of love. This man was the woman's son.

Ethundrel stood back, shocked. The dream was not a dream. What did this mean? He turned more pages. The man was in all the pictures. His importance dominated everyone. There were many men subdued to him. There were bigger and stronger monsters.

The pictures blurred and faded. Things were adding up in Ethundrel's mind. The room reeled about him. All the years he had spent alone, for what purpose? The time he had spent watching from the tower without ever seeing another human had seemed pointless – but now?

This dream – this vision – a message- perhaps the reason that he alone had been spared. He had thought it a punishment of some sort to suffer the endless loneliness but with a sudden exaltation he realised there was a link, some sort of channel from him to her. The book came to an end but he knew it was only a beginning and he knew what came next. The importance of his own continued existence crumbled before the sudden belief that if he concentrated really hard, if he could only show her, maybe the book would never be written.

Allie came out of the supermarket, mentally counting the ingredients for her chicken casserole, reminding herself to get back to the office by two, when he was there in her mind and she froze on the pavement.

He looked straight at her across the dim mist in the treetops and she thought she must be dreaming again, but the weight of the shopping in her bag and the noise of the traffic all around rooted her in reality. Fear raced through her at this daylight invasion. His great eyes seemed to search blindly for her and she softened as she saw despair hiding there. He was trying to tell her something.

She remembered Portia Vane's advice to listen, re-assured herself that he meant her no harm. Fear receded as pictures began to unreel in her mind. It was as if she could see his thoughts, his world. Her surroundings faded as she looked in horror at the burning, dangerous sun, the stunted sickly plants, the deadly stillness of the landscape. She felt his anguish at the silence, the loneliness and her heart welled to help him, all fear forgotten.

He took her down the steps, through the echoing building. His memories came wordlessly, with all the sorrow of past struggles and future hopelessness, then he opened the book and she sensed his dread of the brazen cross that hung above him, felt the woolly dust tickle her nostrils, took the shock as she looked at the pictures of herself, one of Rick, lined and wrinkled beside the young man who shone so fair and zealous. There were tears now in the great round eyes, and the dwarfish hands pulled down the cowl so that she could see the bald, scabby head in all its ugliness.

'What do you want from me?' She threw the words into the pool of images, for a second shattering the pleading from those haunting eyes, then all at once she understood and her hand flew to her stomach.

'My baby! He wants my baby!' She turned in panic, trying to avoid the kaleidoscope of pictures that crowded grimly, pressing on her brain, her body. She tottered away. She must escape, save her child. 'You were wrong' she thought viciously at Portia Vane.

'Get away!' she hissed at the horrid figure that was at once pathetic and terrifying. She began to run, heard a blaring noise and looked up in surprise to see the monster face of a great red bus rearing and roaring over her.

At the top of the tower, stones crumbled and fell. Ethundrel howled in horror and triumph as the world began to waver.

Ethundrel opens his eyes to scintillating sunshine, Parakeets chatter in the bushes outside his window. The metropolis gleams in the distance, insubstantial in the heat haze that hovers over it yet the city is solid, its life is his life. His heart beats daily to its rhythms, in his work, in his familiar haunts, the theatres, restaurants, the coffee shops.

But today is different, his sister Caladriel's wedding day. Today everything is brighter, sweeter, more beautiful than ever, despite, or perhaps because of, the dark stain that lurks at the edge of his mind, an elusive memory of a woman, some strange dream.

But here she comes, his sister in her wedding finery and the other, wrapped in her dim cloud is banished from his thoughts as he gasps at Caladriel's beauty.

At first there is only the emptiness in her belly. The room is white but Alllie's thoughts are the red of blood, the black of death. Rick comes in pale as the grey of his suit, a bunch of freesias bright in his hand.

'Darling,' he says, then his voice breaks and she wants to comfort him but she can only curl inwards like the lost baby, protecting herself and she suddenly remembers the awful staring eyes, the scarred terrifying face and her cry is something not quite human. She can't remember who he was or why he wanted to hurt her and she looks fearfully round the room but he's not there, he is no longer in her mind and she is alone. She wants to tell Rick but he has left the room with the doctor and she knows he will not believe her. They will think she is mad and want to keep her here when all she wants is to go home. She can hear Rick and the doctor talking outside the door, hears the doctor telling Rick, 'no real damage….my advice is to wait a little while…try for another baby.'

When Monsters Turn Real

Saturday's usually the best but this day I got no one to play with. My mate Billy's gone t'pictures with his mam and dad. My mam says we can't afford to go and I'm getting in her way while she's finishing up her cleaning so that's why I'm mooching around on Ashurst Beacon on my own.

It's hard pushing the bike up the steep slope. I'm puffing and wondering whether Mam'll get me the Action Man I want for Christmas when I get the idea to go to Scary Mary's. The hill flattens out a bit and I can get back on the bike and ride lazy up to Brow Lane. Just as I'm going to turn in, a red Mini Cooper flies past and I stop to watch and one day I'm going to have one only mine's going to be racing green, then I'm going down the lane and it's right narrow even now but in the summer the cow parsley grew so tall along the edges it almost met in the middle. Dad says Action Man is a dolly and only for cissies and no son of mine is going to have one but I reckon Mam'll talk him round.

I nearly miss the gate to Scary Mary's farm, hiding round the bend in the lane and have to pull up quick so the bike skids on soggy leaves and I nearly go over the handlebars. I put the bike behind a gorse bush. There's a little stream that runs out by the gate and I always stop to have a look in case there's anything in there, but it's just water and stones and mud and such and I think how I never been here before on my own, Billy's always been with me and I feel a bit scared but then I think how I can brag to everyone in school on Monday how I went up to Scary Mary's front door all by myself and rung the bell and didn't even run away till she opened it.

I'm halfway up the straggly path before I realise it and it's only when I've tripped over a few hidden stones and tree roots that I remember to look out the land properly like Action Man would or the Indian scouts in the Westerns on telly. There's not so much to hide behind now it's nearly winter but I manage to squat down behind the clumps of brambles and an old rotting cart while I case the farmyard, just in case Scary Mary's in the barn or the old stone lavvy round the side of the house; just in case she comes charging along with the shotgun

70

everybody knows she's got. I come to a place where there's no cover and I'm a sitting target so I sneak over to one of the chicken sheds that never have any chickens and I hide round the side of it and sneak looks at the farmhouse to try and see if Scary Mary's inside. Nothing moves, not even any birds; everything here is dead and falling to bits, the house, the carts and ploughs lying round, even the barn is full of mouldy rotten straw that's been there as long as I can remember. Sometimes me and Billy find mushrooms and things growing in it and there used to be mice but even they don't go there any more. I notice this chicken shed is the only thing that looks like it wants to carry on standing up and that's only because someone, Scary Mary I suppose has nailed loads of planks all over it to hold it together. It's so quiet it's creepy and just as I think it's safe to make a dash across the yard I hear a noise coming from inside the shed and it's a rattly grunting beastly noise that makes the hair on my neck stand up. For a minute my heart stops 'cause I think it's Scary Mary but then I know it can't be; there's a big padlock on the door and she can't lock herself in, can she?

We've been here loads of times and we never heard nothing in here before and I try to climb up to the blacked out windows but I can't reach up that high and they're all painted out anyway so's you can't see nothing and whatever it is starts up a racket when it hears me scraping my feet on the boards and it starts screeching and throwing itself against the door and I'm so scared I fall off the planks I'm hanging on and bash my knee on the floor and I don't even feel it 'cause I'm working out how big the thing must be to be making a noise like that and shaking the wood as it bounces against the door. I reckon it must be as big as the sow Mrs Atherton keeps in her back garden and I figure that must be what it is and I don't feel quite so scared as long as it can't get out and trample all over me. Still I wish Billy was here and when there's another crash at the door I'm ready to run away but I stop because the noise it's making is changing and it's almost as if there are words in the screeching even though I know that can't be.

I stand still and listen and it goes 'sto….sto…sto…nomo or nono….sto..stot…' over and over again, noises that don't mean owt but just the same they're not just noises. I think it must be a parrot but there's another big crash at the door so I know it must be bigger than an eagle and it's a giant or a monster like Frankenstein or one of those creatures from outer space that just want to kill everyone on the planet. I know it's going to break out in a second and get me and my legs are like jelly and I can't do nothing and it's still going 'sto..st..sto…nono…nomo…nomo' and suddenly I'm running and I don't even think about Scary Mary and I'm through the farm gate and pedalling up the lane as fast as I can go past the pub. I don't stop till Scarclough church comes round the corner and our school and then it's like coming out of the flicks on a sunny afternoon, everything's twice as real as usual and Billy's dad's Vauxhall is parked outside their house and there's me mam standing at our door looking out for me and she shouts at me like she's pretending to be cross, 'Lord look at the state of you, what have you been up to Jimmy?' I can't say nothing 'cause I can't get me breath I been riding so hard and I can feel my face all red and I'm huffing and puffing. She's pulling me inside as soon as I've got off the bike and I get to gasp out, 'Mam there's a monster in Scary Mary's shed.'

'Oh you and your storytelling,' she says and she shoves me along the lobby. 'I've told you afore how many times not to go mithering Mary Appleton.'

'But there is I heard it.'

' Now you get on and wash your hands, your tea's on the table.'

In the scullery I splash cold water on my face and hands and that makes me feel better and now I'm home and everything's just like it always is, the monster seems to get smaller and I'm just in time for Dr Who and there's beans on toast for tea. I forget all about Scary Mary and the thing in the shed and after Dr Who, it's time for me to get a bath and then Mam's watching Morecambe and Wise and I'm drawing a Dalek when Dad comes home from the pub. Mam gets his tea and gives me a mug of cocoa and a couple of Rich Teas and Dad comes in from the kitchen and says, 'What's all this about you messing round at Appleton's?'

' There's a monster in her shed,' I say, hoping that'll put Dad off giving me a leathering 'cause I know Appleton's is out of bounds.

'You keep away from there me lad,' says Dad, 'she's nutty as a fruitcake.'

' Now Dan,' Mum says, 'she's just a rekloos. She likes to mind her own business.'

'Whatever she is he better keep away.'

'But the monster,' I say and I'm starting to get shaky again 'cause Dad is nearly as scary sometimes as Mary Appleton.

'And you better stop making up stupid stories,' Dad roars, 'what with Daleks and space ships now it's monsters in sheds.'

I don't get leathered but I get sent to bed early but I can keep the light on and read my Eagle annual so I don't mind, even though I've read it twenty times already and I hope I'll get a new one this Christmas. I wonder what a rekloos is and if that's why Mary Appleton is scary and I think it's maybe one of those god people, not a nice one like Mr Forshaw the vicar but one of them that comes up from the new town down the hill where they all live together in a sort of housing estate just for them with a kind of church thing in the middle. They all bash bibles, Dad says, and maybe that's why poor Mary's nutty as a fruitcake. I wonder again if Mam's got my Action Man yet; she starts buying things for Christmas around September right after she's got my school uniform......

Monday morning I'm in trouble at break time. I got an A for composition and Miss Ashton read my story out to the class so even though it were a good story all about a man from Mars who gets trapped in London, everybody hates me except Billy.

'Teacher's pet! Teacher's pet!' they're all shouting, even while we're drinking our milk and afterwards while me and Billy are playing aeroplanes and trying to look like we don't care, just about the whole class comes over, even the girls.

Norman Forster's in the lead of course. He's the richest kid in the village, he's got every Action Man since they first come out and his dad used to be a butcher but now he has a load of butcher's shops and he don't butcher no more, just drives around telling all the other butchers what to do. The Forsters live in Beacon House which is a new house, bigger than all the other houses for miles, at the end of the village on the way down to Parbold.

I wish my dad were rich like that but then I look at Norm and think I wouldn't want to be him even if he has got all the latest Dinky space models. He hasn't really got any friends, not like me and Billy; but today they're all on his side and today is definitely pick on Jimmy day. They're all chanting, 'teacher's pet,' and coming closer, bunching up and when the girls drop back behind the marked lines of the netball pitch, that's when me and Billy know the boys are going to attack so we zoom off still being aeroplanes towards the old air raid shelter where we can see Mr Roper talking to Miss Ashton and he's supposed to be on playground duty but he's only looking at her all mushy. We all know he's sweet on her but she don't seem to want to know and he's so busy looking at her he doesn't see Norman Forster run at me and I can't call out because snitching is the worst thing so I zoom out of the way, my arms stiff out on either side and Norm runs right into Billy and knocks him flat to the ground.

Now I can't run away and leave Billy and the rest of them are making a ring round me and forcing me back against the grass hump of the shelter and I look up and Norm's coming at me with his fists up and I can see Billy getting up with a bloody nose and I'm trying to think what Action Man would do or even James Bond. I got to play for time somehow and before I know it, out of the blue I say, 'I know summat you don't. I know a secret,' and Norm stops in his tracks 'cause he likes to think he's cock of the school and knows everything that goes on. He's still got his fists up but he says all sneery like, 'what do you know you great crate-egg?' And I know I got him 'cause he's forgot he's supposed to talk posh, not like the rest of us so I don't feel so scared when he laughs at me and spits on the floor. 'Tha knows nowt,' he says and turns to the others and they laugh too.

'Do too. I know a secret you don't know.'

'Tell or I'll knock yer block off.'

He's a lot bigger than me and everyone goes quiet waiting to see if he's going to hit me so I blurt out, 'There's a monster in scary Mary's shed.'

'Ah bollocks.' He spits on the floor again and looks at me as if I'm a piece of dog shit.

'There is too. I heard it a Saturday.'

He looks at me and I can tell he don't believe me but he ent quite sure. He grabs Billy by the shirt.

'You see it?' He pushes his face close up to Billy's bloody nose and Billy shakes his head. His eyes are watering but he's trying not to cry.

'I were on my own,' I say quiet. There's a gasp all round and Norm goes, 'Go on, you never went to Scary Mary's on your own,' but everyone is looking at me like I'm someone important like the grownups look at Mr Forshaw in church on Sundays and I start to feel better.

'Did too,' I say, 'and I were hiding round the chicken shed to see where she were and I heard the monster inside. It were big and it were trying to get out.'

'It'd be a goat,' says Charlie Massom who don't believe in space monsters.

'Or a piggy wig,' says Norman and laughs.

'Weren't, I say, 'it talked.' Now they're all quiet.

'Talked?' Norman laughs again but he knows he's on a sticky wicket by the way everyone's watching only me. 'What'd it say?'

'Dunno. Some funny language. Told you – it's a monster – from outer space.'

Norm steps back. 'Why doesn't it come out?' asks Charlie.

' 'Cause it's locked in. Scary Mary caught it and locked it up. Maybe she's waiting for its brothers to come and get it in a space ship and maybe she's going to go up in the sky with them and no one'll ever see her again.'

Everyone's got their mouths open, even Norm, even Billy, then Norm shakes himself, closes his mouth and grabs my tie.

'Right Jimmy Liar. You're gonna come with us and show us this monster after school. Right?' He turns to the circle and they all shout back, 'Right,' but some of them don't sound too keen. After school? I hadn't thought of this. It'll be going dark.

'Me mam says I have to go straight home.'

'Oh, Mam says, Mam says. I say you're going to show us. Show us what a liar you are and if it ent there I'm gonna knock yer block off.'

The bell goes for class and Mr Roper hurries over and starts shooing us back in and I think what a mess of trouble I've got myself in now and I'm so busy thinking about it that I miss most of the geography lesson and Miss Ashton makes me stay in at dinnertime to catch up.

All afternoon I think about making a run for it at half-past-three but I can't because the first thing Norman does is to grab Billy when we get outside the school gate and I can't leave him so I trail along as Norm frogmarches Billy up the hill to Brow Lane and out of all the boys only Charlie Massom and Loony Lewis come along. Charlie probably thinks I'm imagining it's a monster and wants to see what it really is and Loony Lewis goes anywhere anyone else is going. Dad says he was dropped on his head but Mam says he was born like that but he's nearly always happy so what does it matter?

It's a bright day but the sun's dropping as we come up the Beacon road to the top of the hill. It's a long way to Brow Lane on foot and it's just starting to go dark when we creep through Scary Mary's gate and the path up to the farm is spooky in the sort of mist that's trying to form. It's cold and the overgrown bushes look like the triffids in the film I saw on telly last week and I wouldn't admit it to no one but I'm pretty scared and the more I look the more I think I can see those bushes move. Everyone is quiet and Norm lets go of Billy now while he's looking round like he can see the bushes moving too but Billy's too scared to run away and the four of us bunch together. Even Loony Lewis catches the scary feel and huddles close to my back. I cheer myself up imagining I'm in the jungle chopping paths with my machete and zapping Japs as they pop out of bamboo thickets.

'I want to wee,' says Loony Lewis and his voice makes us all jump.

'Shut up,' Norman hisses. 'Go over there.' He points to a clump of brambles and we wait, listening to Lewis's piss pattering on the leaves.

We stop at the edge of the yard. The farmhouse is black, no lights on though it's almost dark now, too dark to see properly indoors. I wonder if Scary Mary's sitting in there in the dark. I never been here in the dark before so I don't know if she has lights like everyone else. Maybe she goes to bed soon as it goes dark like people did in the old days. Next thing I hear a noise, a sort of low moaning and I know we all hear it 'cause we all huddle together.

'What's that,' Norm squeaks out and he looks right scared then tries to pretend he's not by whacking at the nearest bush with a stick he's picked up on the way. Billy's sniffing but I can't see in the dim light if his eyes are watering.

'It's the monster,' I say and now I just want to run away and go home like before, but I can't.

'It's just an animal,' Charlie says but he don't sound too sure.

' I want to go home,' Loony Lewis cries and as his voice echoes across the yard the thing in the shed starts banging and screaming louder than it did before and its going, 'stot stot stot stot,' and kicking and thumping and Loony Lewis screams and suddenly I'm running with my eyes shut and something's tugging the back of my jacket and I don't stop till I almost slip on the cobbles and Loony Lewis crashes into my back where he's been hanging on to me and Billy is crying right next to me. I look round and there's no sign of Charlie or Norm but I can hear crashing noises on the path and I'm standing in the yard right in front of the farmhouse and the front door is wide open and in the dark hall there's a heap of

82

something. Billy pushes me and I take a step in and see the heap has a horrible face, twisted like the worst monster you could ever think of and before I can stop it a great yell comes out of me and I'm backing and running with Billy and Lewis behind me. I don't think about the thing in the shed and I'm screaming so loud I couldn't hear it anyway. I can see the tiny orange lights of the motorway in the distance, behind the chicken shed and I run, we all run out of the farm, wailing all the way down the hill till the church lights hit us.

Dad didn't believe me about the monster but he believes it now when Norman Forster's dad knocks on our door and makes me tell him the whole thing all over again because Norman can't hardly talk for blubbing.

'Two monsters,' I say and Dad gives me one of his looks but he don't say nothing and we all get in Mr Forster's Humber Hawk while the whole street is watching from their front windows.

'If this is another of your fairy stories you're in for a good hiding,' Dad mutters at me over the front seat so even though I never been in a car like this before there's no fun in it what with Dad glaring back at me and Norman snivelling next to me and anyway I don't want to go back there in the dark. Even grownups can't always tackle monsters can they? What if the monsters take us over like that film with the bodysnatchers and no one will know what happened 'cause we'll still look just the same but it won't be us any more?

The car goes down Brow Lane and the beams of the headlights make the darkness even more scary. We don't get out right away because Norman's dad has called the police and says we have to wait for them to come.

I'm so scared I want to pee but I daren't ask and Mr Forster gives Dad a cigarette and they sit there smoking even though the smoke goes up my nose and makes me cough.

'Stop that,' Dad says and he turns round and pokes me in the ribs then another car comes down the lane and it's the police and we all get out. I don't want to but Dad has hold of my arm and he won't let go as we follow the policemen up the path.

'Where is it then lads?' says one of the policemen. Norman stands behind me and I point at the black hole that's the open farmhouse door. 'One's in there,' I say 'and the other's over there.' I turn towards the shed.

Norman's rubbing at his eyes and I can feel my own eyes go wet and I can't stop my lip trembling. Mr Forster puts his arm round Norman's shoulders but my dad pulls me across the yard and I'm thinking, what if they're not there, what if they got up and went away or if someone or something come and took them away? What if they dissolved like the Invaders do or what if they're hiding in the bushes, maybe there's more of them, dozens, hundreds. What if…?

'Sto sto no nono nomo.' We all jump when the banging starts up, even the police and over the thumps we can hear the voice screeching words that aren't words and Dad lets go of my arm and I look up and see he's scared stiff. We get behind the policemen and Mr Forster and Norm get behind us and the policemen shine their torches on the shed and the thing goes quiet for a second then starts up louder than ever.

The policemen try to peep through the cracks in the wood then one says, 'Jesus Christ,' and the other says, 'What is it?' and the first one says, 'I don't know but we don't go in till we get some help.'

We all go to the farmhouse and even before we get near, the light from the torches shows the other monster still huddled on the floor. I grab Dad's arm and hold on tight and Dad goes, 'It's Mad Mary,' and we all stand in a huddle while one policeman goes back to the car to call for help and the other goes closer and shines the torch on the horrible face and I don't believe it's Scary Mary because I seen her lots of times and she weren't never as scary as this.

'Dead,' says the policeman. 'Electrocuted, looks like.' He pokes at a wire on the floor and there's this old vacuum cleaner poking out under Mary's legs.

'You sure?' says Mr Forster. 'Maybe we should try...'

'No,' says the policeman. 'You'd better put your boys in the car. One of you wait with me.' Mr Forster takes me and Norm back to the Humber and gives me a fifty-pence piece and says, 'Don't be scared, Jimmy we'll be going home soon,' and then an ambulance comes and another police car but they can't get Scary Mary's gate open so they all have to walk up the path and after a bit there's a lot of screaming and banging and I forget about what I'm going to buy with the fifty pence and after a while the ambulancemen come down with a bundle on a stretcher and Mr Forster crosses himself and says, 'Poor Mary,' and then two policemen come struggling with a bundle. It's all wrapped up in a blanket and tied round with belts and it must be heavy because they're slipping in the mud and swearing and the thing is wriggling and making these awful noises and we all stare as they go past.

In the light of the torches I can see its head sticking out of the blanket and its mouth is open making those noises, showing lots of sharp teeth and it's covered in hair and its eyes roll around but don't look anywhere. It's like these monsters I saw in a film that lived in caves underground and only came out at night to eat unwary travellers.

It's a worse monster than I could imagine and then Dad jumps in the car and shouts, 'It's a child, oh God it's a child!' and a policeman comes and says, 'Better get these lads home, we'll come and take a statement later,' and Mr Forster drives us home and nobody says anything and when we get home Dad gets the whisky bottle from the parlour and him and Mr Forster have a nip each while Mam gives me and Norman a cup of cocoa.

I try to tell Mam about Scary Mary and the monster but Mam says, 'Hush up and get into your pyjamas,' and she comes and tucks me in which she hasn't done for ages.

I feel better when I'm in bed with my Everton posters round me and the fifty-pence piece under my pillow. I try to think how many sweets I can buy with it but I can't stop thinking about the thing in the shed and how Dad said it were a child but it weren't. It couldn't be.

I hear the Humber Hawk drive off and then Dad comes and sits on my bed and says, 'I'm sorry Jimmy, sorry I didn't believe you,' and I say, 'It's okay,' and Dad kisses me on the cheek which he never, ever does. When he goes away I pick up my Eagle annual but I don't want to read about Dan Dare and the Mekons. I want Mum to come up and read me one of her stories, the one about the princess and the pea or maybe the one about Tom and the water babies.

Paper Money

'Make sure you pay up on time next week.' Jeff turned away from the weeping woman on the step and walked off. Nothing like real paper money, he thought, flicking through his wad of greasy notes; getting rarer these days, everyone dealing in debit and credit cards or online payments. Before long there wouldn't be any real money the way the world was going.

Thankfully, in the world of Jeff's clients, things didn't work like that. Hard cash was all they had and most of it was destined to end up in Jeff's pocket. Losers, every one. They deserved everything they got; borrowing money they couldn't afford, then whingeing, begging for mercy, expecting him to empty *his* pockets for their next trip to the pub or their next packet of fags.

He knocked at Mary Mooney's door, a hard rat-a-tat-tat, just to let her know he meant business. She was way behind with her payments. There was no sound from behind the door but he knew they were in there, her and her two sausage-roll kids. He'd seen that faint twitch of the curtain as he came up the path.

'Mary,' he shouted, 'don't make me lose me temper now.'

He bent and peered through the letterbox. Two soulful brown eyes looked back at him. The youngest Mooney kid was sitting on the floor in a dirty tee shirt and nappy, covered with crumbs, his jaws working on a soggy mess that had once been a pasty; remnants of it mingling with the snot that ran from his nose.

'Jesus,' Jeff muttered, closing the letterbox. He straightened and looked up and down the street. No one round. Good. 'Mary, come on, open up. I'm not going away.' He rattled the flimsy door and then set up a hammering on it. He could hear her coming, stupid tart. She'd try to make excuses, it was the same song every week, but this time she'd have to pay – in cash, or maybe in kind. He didn't get involved with women, they were trouble, just scratched the itch when it started, but Mooney was a good-looking bint with nice tits, even if she was trying to rip him off. He got the itch every time he knocked on her door.

The kid started wailing, then he heard footsteps. He leaned on the doorjamb and waited as he heard the sound of the bolts being drawn, a grin of anticipation spreading across his face.

The door opened and something hit him right between the eyes. His hand went instinctively to the roll of notes in his inside breast pocket but it never got there. When he hit the floor he was out cold.

Nobody made a cunt out of him, nobody. He thought only of what he would do to her when he caught up with her, her and Frisk Stevens. It hadn't taken a nanosecond to find out it was Frisk who'd rolled him. Half the town had seen his unconscious body tipped out of Stevens's beat up old van. He'd been left outside the municipal dump like a sack of garden refuse.

It had started right there; the sniggering, the whispering behind hands but he hadn't noticed then because, more important than that, more important than anything, was the hole at the heart of him where his soul had been torn out. His hand felt inside it, his fingers full of grief as they parted the empty space and crept out again. His hand crawled to his face, laid against his mouth, where he could taste, could smell, the anxious greasy scent of his missing notes. He sighed and looked at the grinning, curious faces above him with murder in his eyes.

Once he'd recovered, he was quick getting round there, calling in Stavros and Kyle on the way but it was too late. He'd known it was too late from the moment he'd opened his eyes. Even a junkie pickpocket and a brainless bitch like Mary Mooney could have figured out that their days were numbered. By the time he got there, they'd well scarpered but he had to smash something if it was only the few battered bits of furniture and the bags of shite they'd left behind.

They'd made a cunt of him all right. It was everywhere he went like the whisper of waves on shingle or a constant backdrop of rain. No one said anything to his face but there was a boldness in their eyes, a disdain in the way they held their bodies away from him, that belied the deference in their voices. He didn't miss a trick; the twitching lips, the quick glances, the air thick with gossip when he came into a room. Yes, they'd made a cunt of him but they wouldn't get away with it.

He pictured over and over how it would be. He'd finish Stevens quickly, he was just a waste of space but he'd take his time with Mary, because of the empty place next to his heart, his bankroll lost, missing like a kidnapped child, already gone for ever, dispersed in heroin dreams and alcoholic hazes, dismembered in crack dens, fractured and fragmented till nothing remained. The pain was worse than a hard kick in the bollocks. Only revenge could burn it away.

'You wanna leave it alone,' Kyle said. 'It's been six months, not a wink. Forget it. Look at you, you're a fucking wreck.'

'Watch who you're talking to,' Jeff growled. 'Money's money. It wasn't yours, was it? How do you think I got where I am? Not through being fucking soft, letting people off, letting knobs like Stevens steal what belongs to me. Do you know what it's like to have to fend for yourself at six years old, drag yourself up by your fucking shoelaces in spite of every fucking bastard that's out to shaft you?'

They were staring at him. He shut up quick, before he spilled his guts. Before the images flooded out of the secret place in his head and poured into his mouth. He wanted to grind his fingers into his eyes, send the pictures back into blackness but he mustn't show weakness. He looked at Kyle and Stavros, their faces were carefully expressionless. They knew nothing. Good lads, but not

93

leaders, not desperate enough for that. Jeff knew one thing – that money was everything, well, money and reputation. He wouldn't stand to lose either.

They must have thought he was a soft touch, thought they could creep back into his manor after a few months and it would all have been forgotten: thought *he* would have forgotten. As fucking if. Before their footsteps had dried on the muddy pavement outside their new rathole, he'd known it. He'd got his cred back in those months, instilling fear into anyone who challenged him, beating the shit out of them if he had to without relying on Kyle and Stavros.

It had been worth it to protect his reputation. The whispers stopped and their loyalty grew like the roll of notes in his breast pocket, so he got the nod before Mooney and Stevens had even closed their rickety front door behind them.

Stevens was easy. There was no chance of getting any money back from a junkie, pointless to try. Jeff, with Kyle and Stavros in tow, waited by the railway arch where Frisk met his dealer. He watched without emotion as the boys waded in, his ears deaf to Stevens's screams. The dealer skedaddled at first sight of them. Jeff didn't have to dirty his hands. Pity they killed the little bastard, Jeff would have liked to have seen him helpless and dependent, shut up in a nursing home with a load of senile wrinklies.

Nothing to worry about though. Who was going to bother about a useless fucker like Frisk floating face down in the canal? Not the cops, that was for sure, one less junkie scum on the streets; a safer life for old ladies and their handbags. Anyway, Jeff was best mates with DI Kenny Simpson, took him out for a posh dinner every once in a while to keep him sweet. There wouldn't be any problems.

Mary Mooney was a different kettle of fish. She would have to pay, for the rest of her miserable life. She'd known better than to run this time, or was it just that she had no fight left in her after what had happened to her boyfriend? He took Kyle and Stavros with him to search the place first, in case she'd found some other cocky little twat who felt like taking a poke at the big man but in view of Frisk's final destination it was hardly likely, was it?

No point bothering to knock, she wasn't going to open the door to him. It only took one good kick and the boys were in, stepping over her kids and cornering her at the kitchen table with her morning bottle of wine.

He stood savouring her terror, it made her more attractive somehow, her dark eyes glossy with fear as Kyle pinned her to her chair while Stavros searched the rest of the house. Jeff felt the itch start up.

'Don't hurt me, don't hurt me,' she kept muttering in that gravelly voice that turned him on. Not a thought for her kids. The baby was howling now, pulling at her leg; the older girl white and silent, stood against the wall glaring at Jeff. Already she knew who was the man.

The kids distracted him. Poor little bastards. For a moment the image came to him of himself in that dingy pokehole he'd shared with his mother, lying shivering under his thin duvet and listening, every sound coming through the rickety walls, stifling his own tears of rage by stuffing his fists in his eyes. He brushed the pictures away.

'Okay boss.' Stavros grinned.

'You can go now,' Jeff said quietly.

Mary Mooney watched them leave. Her fingers played with a safety pin that held her denim shirt closed across her breasts. Her lips muttered endlessly as if she were saying her rosary but nothing came out. Jeff pushed his face close to hers. Her breath whispered on his cheek.

'You owe me, Mary.' He caressed her chin.

She quivered. 'I'll do anything – anything.'

Disgust ran alongside his pleasure. She didn't care about anything, her man, her kids, only her own skin.

'Too right you will. You're going to stay here, just as long as I want you to. No more running. And you're going to pay me back every fucking penny – with interest. It's going to take you a long, long time.'

'Anything,' she ground out.

He squeezed harder. 'You're mine, mine for life. Whenever, whatever I want.' He dropped a hand to her breast.

She quivered again but she looked up and met his stare. A tiny smile curved her mouth.

'Okay,' she whispered.

'Starting now.' He reached in her handbag for her purse with his free hand, took out the single twenty pound note he found there and folded it into his breast pocket. He pulled her to her feet, pressed her against him, felt her yield.

'Not here,' she said detaching the infant from her leg. The small girl pulled the baby away, sat down on the floor with her arms round him. Jeff felt her eyes burning into him. Again his childhood haunted him as he followed Mary to the bedroom. God knows how those kids would grow up, what they had already seen. She should have them taken off her. If he was a respectable man, he'd report her to the authorities, get them into care. It would be the best thing that could happen to them. But then, Jeff and authority didn't mix.

She turned at the bedroom door, gave him a seductive smile. She was already unpinning her shirt, letting him see her breasts. Jesus, what a slapper, but she was stunning and he wanted her. He looked over his shoulder. The two kids were staring at him, the boy silent now, wide-eyed in his sister's arms. He turned away, pushed Mary into the bedroom and closed the door.

He wasn't quite sure when it had started. He wasn't one for running to the doctor with the slightest sniffle.

'Tiredness? Been burning the candle at both ends? Overwork? Too much stress? See it all the time,' the doctor joked.

He was a good doctor, not some clapped out NHS quack.

'Better do a few tests to be on the safe side. It wouldn't do to lose a few pounds.' He peered at the rash on Jeff's stomach. 'Does it itch?'

Weeks later he sat in the waiting room, sweating. Why had he been called in? He wasn't scared, it would be nothing, the doc would give him something for this fucking tiredness. He scratched at the fresh eruption on his neck.

The receptionist smiled at him. She was giving him the eye. No chance. You could tell just by looking at her she'd have you tied up in a pre-nup before you'd get her to open her legs. She wasn't for him. A quick shaft and out was his style and even then, only when necessary. He got more of a buzz from counting his money.

He wasn't a fool. He could see from the doctor's face as he ushered him in, that it was no joking matter.

'Your results are back. It's not good news I'm afraid.'

'Don't beat about the bush.'

'You're HIV positive.'

Jeff's mouth dropped open.

'And unfortunately, you've already developed auto immune deficiency syndrome.'

'AIDS?' Jeff's hand flew to his heart.

'I'm sorry.' The doctor looked at him. 'You must have had unprotected sex?'

'No.' Jeff tried to fathom a brain frighteningly empty. How? How? He only ever used clean girls, no questions

99

asked, from an agency he trusted, and he always used a condom.

An image filled the emptiness. Mary Mooney, that siren smile on her lips, taking a condom from her bedside table and handing it to him, her shirt open, her breasts nosing out, the safety pin still in her hand.

He felt the wodge of his bankroll, reached in his pocket and pulled it out. It was real, solid in his hand.

'Okay doc,' he said, 'how much to get this thing sorted?'

Shoes to Die For

In my dreams he comes to me with eyes as big as teacups. There is red fire in their depths as he thrusts into me and my nose quivers with the keenness of an animal at the rank, sweat smell of the fur on his chest. The howl of his climax is reflected in the moans of the pack outside the door. It is only his humanity that keeps them from bursting in and taking their share.

By day he is smooth-skinned, sweet and supple, sharp-suited, a new man to delight in. The dreams are puffs of smoke soon lost, yet in the mirror I puzzle over claw marks on my nipples.

At work I dream of the red shoes in Baumgartner's window, tapping at my keyboard while my mind strays to dancing, prancing, mincing on those five inch spikes, wickedly scarlet, my legs long as torture, the calf muscles defined. I buy what I can afford, red underwear, red lipstick.

Night falls. Miss Mouse and Mr Wolf dine together on red wine and bloody steaks. He has brought her the gift he knows she craves. He has seen her admiring them in the shop window, has watched his own reflection in the glass over her shoulder, wondered at his face, wild with hair, while his fingers register only the smooth skin of his shaven chin.

In bed he bites into her breasts while she, wrapped round him, admires the red shoes poised on his shoulders, before she drives the spiked heels into his pelt. This time it is her howl that drives the horde outside to frenzy.

This morning there are paw marks in the snow outside the window and teeth marks on my breast. Blood has been drawn and dries in rusty spots on the sheet. Tonight he has promised to take me dancing and the day waltzes slowly past to the appointed time.

Off comes the secretary's skirt and on go black leather and the red shoes. At the Palais, the band is just warming up when he takes me in his arms. I can feel the muscles of his thighs pressed against mine but at the first quick step, the red shoes begin to dance with a life of their own and, locked together we must dance round and round, faster and faster, out of the hall and down the snowy street.

At first I am senseless with excitement at the pressure of his body on mine, flinging myself into the physical rhythm of the dance dictated by the shoes, blood drumming in my veins, but we go higher and higher into the dark, cold forest and I begin to tire. It is so cold, my feet hurt and my legs are whipped by branches and brambles. The red shoes catch on sticks and stones, making me stumble, twisting my ankles, yet ever dancing on and on and he is slipping, sliding from me. I feel his shape shifting till he is on all fours, loping beside me, lupine head raised to the moon.

I am almost done, I cannot breathe and my heart tries to leap into my throat even before the woodsman appears in our path and fires a silver bullet deep into the brain of my beloved.

And now, when horror makes me want away, the red shoes begin to dance me in a circle round the body of my lover, whose hairless skin gleams in the moonlight. His eyes are big as teacups but the red fire has gone. Round and round I go, regretting only my vanity at Baumgarten's window. The red shoes are black with mud.

I want only for it to end and welcome the baying of the pack that now draws close, putting to flight the hovering woodsman who fain would have helped me, thinking me a prisoner of the werewolf.

I am beyond help, my last tottering strength draining into the dancing shoes. The first of the pack bounds into the snowy clearing and stops, his companions close behind. They lick their chops, showing me their bone-crunching teeth. They will avenge their master's death and I will have release.

You Were Made For Me

She's here again. I knew she was coming. My computer told me. When I switched on, I got the message right away. PC, Pat Connors, perfect cunt.

And here she is. Banging on the door. She won't go away, even though I'm hiding behind the curtains, not moving a muscle.

She's shouting through the letterbox. Her words rattle on the vinyl floor, bumping against the walls – big words that crash in the small space.

'LEAVE HIM ALONE.'

That makes me smile. I know what that means. LOVE HIM ALWAYS. I know she doesn't really want him. She wants me to take him away.

There's a little silence. She rattles the letterbox.

'I KNOW YOU'RE IN THERE YOU BITCH.'

She must be bending down now, peering through the flap, looking in my hall to see where her words went. I wish I had a long, hot poker to shove in her eyes, or, better still, to stick in her shouting mouth.

In the kitchen, I switch on the radio to drown out her noise. I'm fed up listening to her. I don't care anymore if she hears me. I know Chris will go mad when he finds out she's been coming here, causing trouble. I know this because on the radio, Cilla Black is singing, 'You're My World.' It's a message from Chris. The words are beautiful and the title is my initials, Yvonne May Waterhouse. See? It's too much of a coincidence, isn't it?

I like the old records. That modern stuff, it's all dance music, loud, toneless sex, sex, sex. I like romance. 10cc is one of my favourite groups. There's another coincidence, cc, Chris Connors, and its ten years since we first met.

I always knew he was made for me, although I kept it to myself for ages. It was only three years ago that I plucked up the courage to tell him, but all that time, I never changed, I never wanted anyone else.

All my life there have been little messages, in songs, in things people say, objects I pick up or look at.

She's gone away now. When I think of all the trouble she's caused, trying to keep me and Chris apart, it's a miracle I can restrain myself from running out and killing her.

It was all *her* fault that I had to leave a good job at the hospital. I'd been ward manager at the general for three years and when Chris came to work on my ward, he was the best staff nurse, I'd had. I knew, that first day, that he was the one, but I didn't let that interfere with my work, whatever they say.

There had been other men before, of course, but I knew someone special was going to come. I was sorry to find out that Chris was married, that he hadn't waited for me the way I'd waited for him, but I knew everything would turn out all right in the end.

He was shy at first, but gradually we got to know each other well as we worked together and I just bided my time until one day it happened just the way I'd always known it would.

Even then, although we couldn't get enough of each other, Chris was always a gentleman. Those filthy things she said, still says, make me sick – things Chris would never do. Ours is a pure love.

We spent every spare minute together. Until she started to cause bother and that's when it all went wrong. Oh, the lies that woman told. She made Chris lie too. I knew he didn't mean it, he was just no match for that scheming bitch.

I could see the longing in his eyes, even when he told me he didn't want to see me any more. I went off shift that night devastated but as I was getting in my car, I heard two women talking in the car park.

'He doesn't mean it dear,' one said to the other. I knew it was a message for me and as I pulled into the town square, I saw the lights of the Kentucky Fried Chicken restaurant, (Kisses From Chris) and the car radio started playing Freddie Mercury singing, 'Carry on, carry on, nothing really matters.' What could I do?

I only went round to Chris's house to try and talk to PC but that woman is just so unreasonable. She just wouldn't understand how fate had brought Chris and I together. I knew it wasn't Chris who sent the police round to my flat, I knew he wouldn't do anything to hurt me. It was Pathetic Cow, and that policeman, Detective Constable Devil's Claw, Clever Dick. He said I threatened her with a knife. It was just a letter opener I found in my pocket. I had to use it to stop her jamming my fingers in the door.

There was a big stink at the hospital after that. They made Chris say he couldn't work with me any more. They said I was sick. They told me to take some time off. Everything was hushed up of course but they wouldn't let me back on my ward. In the end, I resigned and ended up as the matron at this grotty little nursing home.

I couldn't see Chris at the hospital and I couldn't go to the house but I had to let him know that I was still there for him so I tried to ring up instead but PC changed the number after a bit and Clever Dick came round again. Lucky I'd always used a call box so they couldn't prove it was me.

The last few days I've waited for him outside the hospital or outside his house but he won't talk to me because she's always watching. That's why she's been here today, trying to get me through the letterbox.

Time goes better for me at work. Even though this job is a bit of a come down, we're always busy and I can almost forget about not seeing Chris and having to put up with PC and her trouble-causing. I've always loved my job, holding people's lives in my hands. I don't know how I'd manage without it.

But today, just in the quiet time after lunchtime medications, just when I was settling down for a quick cup of tea and a sandwich, the police came – here, to my place of work. How everyone stared. And a detective inspector no less, smooth in a dark suit with a soft, round face.

He said someone had tried to kill PC – pushed her in front of a car on the High Street. At first I was so excited that I didn't really think about what he was saying. All I could see was Chris and me together and an empty space where PC was no more, but his next words crashed into my brain.

'Luckily she wasn't seriously injured, broken wrist…..bruises…..shock.'

I looked at DI. His eyes were cold and flat like the Devil Incarnate. He reminded me of that day, the one I never told about. The suit…it scratched my skin… and the smiling face with the flat, cold eyes….just like this. Funny how a complete stranger can just come up dressed in a suit and a smile and take everything away from you. It was hot that day. I got off the train, cutting through the fields to Aunty Rita's house…the tall grass scratching my legs, then the smile and the suit scratching…then he took the smile off and I saw his real face… so close up….later it was the only thing I remembered.

DI wanted to hurt me too, make everything dirty, everything that is sweet and good between me and Chris.

'What's all this got to do with me?'

He laughed tonelessly. 'Perhaps you could tell me where you were this morning, between say ten-thirty and eleven o'clock?'

'My shift started at nine.' I squared my shoulders.

He was disappointed, I could tell. The staff nurse and the auxiliary backed me up. They'd been so busy they hadn't noticed when I slipped out. It took so little time. I knew what time PC left for work and the route she took. I wanted to laugh out loud when I saw how his face fell. He got up to leave, looked at me like he wanted to call me a liar but I just looked right back. There wasn't a thing he could do.

After he'd gone, I went into the staff room to make a fresh cup of tea. The room was empty. My hands were shaking as I put on the kettle and got my cup. The trailing rhythms of a blues song flowed out of the radio. I listened to the suffering in the voice, in the notes and chords of the guitar and suddenly, I knew I'd had enough.

'That was 'Killing The Blues' by Blind Boy Williams,' said the DJ.

Killing the Blues – it was a message for Detective Inspector Lizard Eyes, DI – Death Instantaneous.

'Mrs Smith needs her insulin,' the auxiliary called me from my reverie. Was it tea-time already? I went into the stock room, unlocked the medicine cupboard, started drawing up the injection. I looked down at the syringe – DI – Death Instantaneous. My eyes slid over the rows of vials – Cubic Centimetres – Chris Connors.

I took two vials. Enough was enough. DI and PC. Their harassment was about to end. PC was still in the hospital. I would have to be careful. Careful and quick. DI first, then PC. After that Chris and I would be together always. I knew I wouldn't get caught. After all, look at this morning. I could get away with anything. I picked up the phone and called the police station.

'Could I speak to Detective Inspector Pearson?' I asked confidently. 'There's something I need to see him about.'

When Did You Last See Your Father?

 Maybe he won't come tonight. Sometimes I'm alone and the house is silent, like it was after the funeral, after they'd all gone home.

'Salt of the earth, your dad, Sandra,' they all kept saying. They looked at me and I remembered I was supposed to be sad when all I wanted to do was to let that wild feeling of relief rip through me.

'Gawn to join your mother,' said Auntie Mabel and I thought, who was Mother? I'd always been Mother for as long as I could remember.

Not any more.

But soon, the empty house started to lean on me. The furniture whispered at me, saying that it was all my fault.

I liked being Mother at first. I felt special. *You're a good girl, Sandra. Just like your mother.'* Just the two of us in the big old house seemed comfy.

But gradually I realised that being Mother was a name for something that other girls didn't do. They didn't do the washing or cook their daddies' dinners. They bought nice clothes and they went to youth clubs and dances. I got to resent the hand on my knee, the step on the stair. *'Good girl, Sandra, come over here.'*

I started to wish he would die. It was the only way it would ever stop.

Mr Brownlow, the vicar, says I mustn't blame myself; it's normal for people to feel guilty after a death, but if that's true, why does he keep coming back?

Just when I thought I was free. I went out that first week and bought myself a new wardrobe. I wore the new clothes around the house but I sensed him everywhere, watching, and when I went to bed, I felt his hands on me and there he was, hot and hoarse, breath sour with tobacco. I went back to my shapeless skirts and sweaters but it didn't help.

'Make him go away,' I begged Mr Brownlow, but he said I was imagining things.

'It was a heart attack; nothing to do with you, Sandra.'

'But he comes every night. He says horrible things to me.' I couldn't say what was really going on.

'You could always sell the house.'

'I've never lived anywhere else. Why should *I* leave?'

Mr Brownlow came and said prayers in the bedroom, but it didn't stop. In fact it got worse, so I'm exhausted every morning and the days drag with nothingness..

Mr Brownlow said I should go to the doctor and the doctor sent me to the hospital. I got here this morning and it's been all right here so far. The nurses are nice and the other patients haven't bothered me, so I thought that I would be safe here.

But now it's night and even here, where other shapes breathe easy and snore, I can hear the squeak of his shoes on the floor and now something is twitching back the sheet.

Ann's Test.

The first day I saw just one, an advance scout. Ann had been gone for two weeks. The next morning there was a whole line of foot soldiers, pointing at yesterday's squashed body like an accusing finger.

I had to get past them. The birds were waiting to be fed. I edged round the door. Nausea rose up my throat at the sight of their shiny black bodies and waving feelers. The pain hiding in my leg bloomed like fire as I limped to the end of the garden to fill the feeders. The ants were from her of course, she'd sent them but why?

I went back to the house. Pain muttered. The ant line was thicker. There was a hole at the bottom of the door through which they were pouring. I bent as low as my hip would allow. They were under a paving stone by the back step.

I hadn't any ant poison. I got the fly spray from the kitchen cupboard. Ants had never invaded before so I knew she had definitely sent them. They didn't die at once, but the spray seemed to clog them up. They began to run in all directions, even up my trouser leg.

I screamed and danced, ignoring my screeching hip. A jar of PanYan pickle on the kitchen worktop shouted to me, 'PanYan, pay Ann.' Oh yes, Ann, you will pay! In the bathroom I tore off my clothes, scrubbing my skin under the shower to get rid of crawly ants' feet and feelers.

I went down to where Ann lives now but Richard came out and told me to clear off.

'BADRATS!' I shouted, waving my crutch. 'BADSTAR!'

'If I see you again, I'll call the police,' he shouted back.

'All right for you Mr Two Legs, wife stealer.'

'Clear off!'

'RAWKEN! BADRATS!' I started to limp away. I thought I saw Ann's face, white against the upstairs window.

'PANYAN!' I shouted up at her, 'PANYAN!'

The next day they were back and I knew Ann wasn't going to give up. There was no fly spray left. Boiling water – I remembered my mother used to use it, but as I filled the kettle, I had a better idea. I used to like Westerns and there was something I'd seen once in a film, or had I read it in a book?

It nearly killed me, lifting that flag. Even with the crowbar, my hip screamed protest and when I saw the horrid, wriggling mass, I nearly fainted. By midday I was exhausted but it was done and everything was ready. Now all I had to do was wait until Ann finished work and Richard got up after sleeping off his night shift.

It was four-thirty when I turned into Ann's street, just starting to go dark. Richard came to the door looking groggy. I tried not to think about what was in my back pack; instead I concentrated on what I needed to do. I had the hammer ready up my sleeve and as soon as his ugly mug peered round the door, I hit him hard.

He staggered back and I followed him in. He looked like a great ugly insect with his eyes bugging out at me, so it wasn't difficult to keep on hitting him.

I dragged him into the front room and shut the door. He'd made a bit of a mess on the hall floor, so I laid a trap for Ann, dipping my scarf in the blood and dripping it on the cream-coloured carpet up the stairs. When I'd finished, I hid behind the bedroom door.

It worked like a dream. I listened to the noise of her key in the lock. There was dead silence as she saw the trail of blood on the stairs. Suddenly she gasped and cried, 'Richie!' then I heard the drumming of her feet up the

119

stairs and she burst into the room. I already had the noose in my hands and she was trussed like a turkey before she even realised what was happening. Once I had her immobile on the floor, I could relax and take my time. As I sat on the floor resting, she began to gabble.

'Where's Rich? What have you done? Mike, why are you doing this? Let me go. You're hurting me. Please, Mike.'

I got more rope out of my bag, just to be safe. I rolled her round and round, tightening the knots. 'Ann's test, nest, test, sent, sent ants,' I explained between gasps.

'What are you talking about? Let me go!'

I got the roll of masking tape. 'Pity me oat. O pity me at. Meat o mate o pity me. TIME TO PAY!' I hissed at her as I wound the tape round her head. I left her nose clear and her eyes so I could watch her reaction when I opened the box.

The pine floor was firm. The nails gave a solid thunk as I hammered them through her hands. Her face looked like it would burst through its sticky covering. It was harder to get the nails in her feet. Luckily she'd fainted by then, but I had to wake her up for the grand finale so I went and fetched a jug of cold water to bring her round.

I opened the box with a shudder of horror, watching Ann's eyes widen. I tipped the box and the squirming mass fell on her face. I fished out the tin of syrup and dribbled it all over her body. That would keep them busy for a while. I went home, savouring Ann's punishment.

I never meant to kill her. I just wanted to make her stop tormenting me. I was going to go back after a couple of days and set her free but my hip was so bad after all my exertions that I had to stay in bed for a week and then people broke in and brought me here, where at least it is clean and safe.

This place is called after St Anne. If you put in a hero, myself of course, you get 'no ants here.' Funny that, isn't it?

My Baby

Soon as I set eyes on him I knew I had to have him. It was those navy blue eyes and the sleepy mouth, just a little bit open, and the way his hair wisped up from his head. He just lay there, arms and legs akimbo, like he was ready for the best sleep ever.

'I got to have him,' I says to Kev.

'Don't be a dickhead,' Kev says, 'Two hundred and seventy quid. You having a laugh, Elaine?'

'Oh I know,' I says, but when he went to the toilet I sneaked back to the stall with my credit card and then I had him in my arms and Kev couldn't do nothing about it, could he?

'What'll we call him?' I says to Kev in the car on the way home.

'Whatever you bloody like. How about daylight robbery?' His knuckles were white on the steering wheel and he wouldn't look at me.

'No, you choose,' I says, 'cos I was thinking Kev's going to be his dad so he ought to have a say in what he's going to be called, give him a sense of responsibility. 'Go on.'

'I dunno. Sam, Tom, Dick, Harry.'

'I was thinking Marco,' I says, but then I thought Marco's kind of Spanish or Italian and he's going to be a proper English little boy with those blue eyes and blond hair. I thought about Harry for a minute but he wasn't a Harry.

'What about William,' I says, 'we can call him Wills, like he's royal.'

'More like a ciggie,' Kev says and he starts laughing, 'them ones me dad used to smoke, you know, Woodbines.'

I didn't get it and I didn't think it was right laughing at Wills like that and I told him so.

'It's a doll, Elaine,' Kev says.

But he's so real, I thought. I could see Kev was getting mad, he was driving too fast and throwing the car round corners. I thought he would have to be more careful driving now we'd have a baby in the car and I picked Wills up and held him tight.

That night he slept in the wicker basket I kept for my ironing, good as gold, not a whimper. The lady I bought him from had given me a bag of goodies for him, little things – dummies, booties, a little rattle and a card with dates of stalls she was having at other fairs.

'Look Kev,' I says, 'there's a doll and pram fair in Manchester next Saturday.'

'Forget it,' Kev says, 'no chance. I must've been crazy to let you talk me into going into that one today.'

'It was fate,' I says, looking at Wills lying there so sweet. I never thought about dolls before, didn't even like them as a kid – and what made us go to Lytham today, somewhere we hardly ever go? What drew us to the doll fair in the theatre? It was meant for Wills to find me, we were just right for each other, that's why he was so contented now, even though he'd only been with us a few hours.

The next day I went out and bought a cot and all the other little things Wills needed; vests, nappies, babygros, bottles, steriliser, jumpers, pants and the cutest little blue coat. At home he had his first bath and went to bed without a murmur. Kev went mad when he came home from work and saw all the things.

'Kev,' I says, 'I don't know what you're getting so cross about – after all, this time we won't be packing the things up for the charity shop or giving them away to one of the neighbours whose daughter's having a baby.'

Kev didn't have no answer to that. He just looked at me and went to the pub without eating his supper. I didn't mind that, though. I was hungry for time to be alone with Wills but I didn't wake him up. Babies need their sleep and a regular routine. I had a wonderful time folding all his clothes and arranging them in the little chest in the spare room. I hadn't liked to go in there for ages but now things were different.

The room was painted primrose with a frieze of little rabbits running round the middle but it would be better painted blue. I'd get Kev to do it when he was in a better mood. Wills's cot was in our bedroom for the time being. I thought it best to keep him there until we were used to each other – bonded. I twirled the mobile over his head and his eyes seemed to follow the coloured shapes and then he looked at me and his lips puckered into a smile.

On Saturday morning, I got up early while Kev was asleep. I took the car and drove to Manchester. Kev would be mad but I didn't care. Wills slept all the way in his Moses basket. I kept thinking how lucky I was that he was such a good baby. When I got to the place where the fair was being held, I took Wills out of his basket and put him in the baby carrier I got with his other things. The weight of him felt so good strapped against my chest, his little body snuggled against me.

There were lots of other babies at the fair but none as cute as Wills. The prams were wonderful, lovely old-fashioned ones, with shopping baskets and parasols; nice big prams a baby could lie down in or sit up and play with his toys and facing forwards so he could see his mummy, not like those horrible buggy things they have nowadays.

I felt really at home there among all the other mums who were pushing their babies round and I was glad me and Wills had come on our own. Kev would only have been in the way. There was a beautiful black Silver Cross pram, I kept looking at it but it was a twin.

'It's a rare model,' the lady on the stall said.

'But I've only got the one,' I said, patting Wills on the back. He was getting heavy and starting to wiggle and grizzle.

'He's a gorgeous boy,' she said, coming round to the front of the stall. 'He'd look lovely in here,' she turned back the apron on the pram to reveal pale blue frilly pillows and quilt. 'I'll even throw the bedding in for free.'

127

'But I've only got the one,' I said again, looking at the six-hundred-pound price tag.

'You'll be wanting another,' she leaned forward to touch Wills's cheek. 'A little sister. I bet he'd love that.'

'I don't want another.' I pulled Wills away from her probing finger. I didn't want anyone else touching him. 'I'd better go; it's time for his feed.'

I could feel her staring after me as I made my way to the toilets. In the cubicle I sat on the pan and held Wills close.

'There's only you, darling,' I promised him. 'There'll never be another baby.' He was clinging to me because of what that stupid woman had said. 'It's all right, sweetheart.' I started to sing a lullaby and gradually he relaxed against me, his head nuzzling my breast. It just felt right to pull up my jumper and let his mouth find my nipple. After all, that's what it was made for.

We went home with a grey Royale pram. It had little restrainer straps inside for when Wills was ready to sit up and I knew that wouldn't be long, he was such a bright little boy. Already he was starting to talk. In the car on the way home, he distinctly said, 'Mama,' and all the time he was watching me with those knowing blue eyes.

Having the pram meant I could take Wills for long walks and show him off round the town but I had to hide it in the shed and wait till Kev had gone to work before venturing out. I was so proud wheeling him round the shops with people stopping to peep in at him and say how beautiful he was. Most people, that is, except for a few nosey parkers like old Mrs Rogers.

'Didn't even know you was pregnant again,' she says, looking me up and down.

'His name's Wills,' I says, trying to get between her and the pram but I wasn't quick enough.

'Is that a real baby?' she says, poking a dirty finger at Wills so I had to knock her hand away for fear of him getting her germs.

'Have to go,' I says, 'feeding time,' and I pushed past her and walked back home quick as I could because it wasn't a lie, Wills was waking up and starting to wail for his dinner. He was a good baby but ever so greedy, he seemed to want feeding every half an hour. Soon as I got in and got him out of his pram, his little fingers were squeezing at my breast. I was getting tired out with it all and that made me snappy with Kev. It didn't help when the credit card bill came in and Kev went ballistic.

'Nine hundred pounds you've spent on all this crap,' he waved at Wills's basket, his toys, the clothes I was ironing.

'They're all things Wills needs,' I says.

'It's a doll, Elaine,' Kev yelled. 'You're going to bankrupt us over a fucking toy.' He started punching the wall and it made me jump and Wills woke up in his basket.

'Don't exaggerate,' I says and I went to pick Wills up but Kev got in front of me and started shouting. 'We're overdrawn, Elaine, we can't pay the sodding mortgage!' He went to grab Wills but I got there first.

'Don't you dare,' I says and I took Wills into the bedroom. He was shaking with fright. 'It's all right, little lamb,' I says and I gave him my breast.

Kev came bursting in. 'Elaine, what the hell do you think you're doing?' His eyes were all funny and his face looked green.

'You frightened him,' I says and I went on rocking Wills.

'I'm going for the doctor,' Kev says and he barged out of the house.

Wills let go of my nipple and looked up at me. 'Mummy?' he said and that's when I knew that me and

Wills couldn't stay in the house with Kev. It just wasn't safe.

'It's reaction after the miscarriage,' the doctor says when he finally turned up.

'But that was nearly a year ago,' Kev says.

'These things can take a long time,' the doctor says and he came over to me. 'Let me take the baby,' he says and I didn't want to but I let him because he was the doctor and maybe he ought to check Wills over.

'Maybe a few days in hospital,' the doctor says and he put Wills back in his cot.

'No,' I says, 'I'm not going. I got to look after Wills.'

Kevin started huffing but the doctor gave him a look. 'Perhaps a short course of diazepam – just to calm things downs a bit – and something to help you sleep? Your husband tells me you don't get much sleep.'

'Well who does with a young baby?' I says and the doctor nodded and smiled and wrote out a prescription and Kev went off to the chemist's with it. I wanted to say that I didn't want no pills but I thought it was better to have the pills than the hospital so I didn't say nothing when Kev came back with the tablets. I didn't even say nothing when Kev says, 'You'll have to get rid of that doll, Elaine,' but I crushed the tablets up and put them in

131

a curry and gave it to Kev for his supper and then me and Wills had a long bath and when we came out Kev was asleep in front of the telly so I gave Wills his last feed and we both went to bed.

Sometime in the middle of the night I woke up and Wills's cot was empty and right away I knew Kev had taken him and I ran out in a panic, my head flapping, thinking of my poor little baby dumped all alone somewhere out in the dark and cold, but Wills was sitting up at the top of the stairs and Kev was lying at the bottom. One look told me his neck was broken.

I rushed to pick Wills up but something in his eyes stopped me. 'What have you done?' I started to cry for poor Kev who hadn't been so bad really. But Wills wouldn't answer. He lay back with his arms and legs akimbo, his navy eyes, darker than ever, turned up to the ceiling. He looked like he was ready for the best sleep ever.

Dinner

This meal is important for John. I have to remember that. The room is hot. The white tablecloth dazzles me. I'm relieved to see there is a large jug of water on the table. I pour myself a glass, slowly, carefully, so I won't knock it over. The cold touch of the glass keeps me steady, focussed.

John is fussing over his boss's wife. She's fat, much fatter than me. I can take off my jacket, show the snug waistband of my skirt. I look round the room. It's full of warm, noisy faces, moist open mouths, clinking cutlery, laughter, mumbling, mouthing, chewing, slurping. There is no food on our table. Yet.

My handbag is by my feet. The calorie counter is inside. I pick up the menu too quickly. John gives me a look. I remember my promise and smile at Oliver, the boss. I let my finger stray down the list of food, soupcons of this, pan-fried that, soused in something, flamed with grease, covered in cream clots, soaked in snot, smothered with vomit, drenched in piss…

I want to jump up, in fact my legs jerk in preparation. John is looking at me. A waiter comes, puts down a dish of bread and licks his pencil. I look at the stodgy doughy stuff and get up too quickly, pulling the tablecloth in my haste. John looks aghast, but it is all right, my hand, still clenched round the glass, stops me spilling the water.

'Must nip to the loo.' I want to put on my jacket, grab my bag and run, but I don't. It's too important to John, so I just pick up my bag, slowly, carefully and make myself saunter to the ladies' room.

In the cubicle, I get out the calorie counter and look at the picture of Julia Judge on the cover. Slim, neat, calm, sophisticated. If only I could be like her.

When I come out, another woman is standing at the sink, washing her hands. She's older than me and she's fat, so fat that she takes up nearly all the room in the small area.

I hide my disgust and wash my hands, looking in the mirror at the waistband of my skirt, looking for bulges under my tight fitting top.

'Nice place this, dear, isn't it?' The woman is old, someone's grandmother. I remember my grandmother like a bloated whale in her coffin.

In the mirror I can see fat collecting along my hips. On the day my grandmother was buried my father said to my mother.

'No wonder she had a stroke. All that blubber. You'll be the same if you're not careful.' His lip curled as he spoke.

I don't want to have a stroke. I slide my hands down my hips.

'I don't really like restaurants,' I tell the woman. 'I don't have much appetite.'

'You're a skinny little duck, aren't you?' She is combing her hair now. Her hair is thin and faded. She pulls it forward to frame her fat, flabby face. Her cheeks hang. I feel I could poke my finger through the dangling flesh without any resistance. I run my finger over the taut line of my cheekbone and turn my face side on to the mirror.

'Been poorly, have you?' She looks my reflection over, my reflection that I hope is fatter than reality.

'I'm fine,' I say and it comes out sharp and nasty, surprising us both. Her mouth is open, I can see her teeth, false teeth, waiting to chomp and mash. I want to escape, but she's blocking the door and I remember that food will be arriving now on the table, back in the restaurant, heaped plates like steaming piles of shit.

John will have ordered for me and whatever it is I shan't be able to eat it and he will be angry. My stomach swells just at the thought of it and I can feel the waistband of my skirt tighten. I'm caught between a rock and a loaded table. What would Julia Judge do?

My arms and legs feel twitchy. The little room and the fat woman are squashing me.

'Excuse me,' I say and make a grab for the door. I have to push past the woman and I can see that she is staring and I know Julia would want me to be calm and to walk slowly, carefully, but I can't.

I'm still thinking about the fat woman as I rush out of the rest room and collide with a waiter carrying two plates of pasta. He twirls with the dishes above his head, reeling off course but miraculously regains his balance. How did he do that? I stop in admiration, till I realise people at the nearest tables are staring at me.

Across the room John is deep in conversation with his boss. He hasn't noticed, or so I think until I make my way to the table. Oliver's wife Sylvia is looking me over. I smooth the waistband of my skirt. Is she envious of my figure or can she see the fat I can now feel coating my hipbones?

John is looking up at me between sentences, sly glances under his shaggy eyebrows. I can see by the tightness of his smile that he is full of anxiety. He's waiting for me to make a fool of myself. I pick up the menu again.

'I've ordered you a salad for starters.' John sounds nervous. I want desperately to get the calorie counter out of my handbag but I mustn't. My fingers shake. The menu rattles in my hands. Sylvia looks at me with raised eyebrows. I can smell hot, horrible, foody smells; garlic, meat, frying chips.

On the next table a man cuts into a bloody steak. I feel sick. John's eyes bore into me. I put my hand round my glass of water. The cool cylinder concentrates my attention. I lift the glass carefully and sip the water, resisting the urge to slurp and slobber it down. My stomach fills and I feel stable. I know Julia is smiling approvingly in the darkness of my handbag.

Sylvia's starter arrives. Stuffed peppers and garlic bread. It stinks. I open my mouth to tell her garlic bread has 300 calories a slice and I see John's warning look, so I cover my mouth with my hand and pretend to yawn. I top up my glass of water. The jug rattles against the rim. I hold the glass steady with my right hand. John is looking at my left hand. My left hand is writing 300 over and over on the tablecloth with such force that my nails have indented the number on the fabric.

'Of course we'll expand our European markets,' John says to Oliver, although he can't stop looking at my fingers. The waiter plonks a plate before me with a flourish. There are a few salad leaves, a slice of something dead and a bilious trail of dressing.

'Come on now, no more talking shop in front of the girls.' Oliver covers Sylvia's free hand with his and winks at her. Sylvia's other hand rams forkfuls of pepper and stuffing into her mouth. She smiles, too busy gobbling to reply.

'What are you having?' I ask John. If I talk it puts off the moment of eating.

'Smoked salmon for both of us,' Oliver answers as the plates arrive. The salmon looks like wet orange paper. Was it once a leaping, living thing that revelled in its wetness, its affinity with and separateness from the water?

I push the things round on my plate, select the least revolting, a slice of radish and cut it into manageable pieces. John kicks my foot under the table. Don't – I beg with my eyes.

'We'll have the Australian Chardonnay,' Oliver tells the waiter. He drives his fork like a power tool, expertly rolling up the salmon and lifting it to his glistening mouth. His fat white fingers pull at the bread. Does he pull at Sylvia the same way?

She is patting her mouth with her napkin and watching as I struggle to pick up a tiny piece of radish on my fork. At last I must put it in my mouth and manage to keep it there. It lies on my tongue, sending out messages of coolness contradicted by spicy heat. Juice squirts in the bottom of my mouth, under my tongue like a flood in a cellar. I swallow the piece quickly, close my eyes and swill down half a glass of water. Oliver pours the Chardonnay.

'How's your salad?' says John.

'Fine.' I admire the bubbles in the yellow wine although I know I won't be able to stomach the taste. They have all finished eating and watch as I pick up another square of radish.

'They do a lovely salad at Antonio's on the High Street,' says Sylvia encouragingly, cradling her wineglass in her fingers. Her fingernails are the colour of rotten peaches.

I wonder if John has told them about my little problem. Do I see pity in her expression? The radish square is sticking on my tongue. Chew your food thoroughly, is Julia Judge's advice. I masticate while the others consult the menu yet again.

I choose the safest dish – vegetable and pasta parfait. John looks relieved.

'Must leave room for my dinner.' I push my plate away and pat my mouth like Sylvia. There is a short silence and the full gastronomic cacophony of the restaurant breaks over me.

Everywhere I look I can see wet mouths and sharp teeth. Faintness nibbles at the edge of my mind at the thought of the heap of food I will shortly be expected to eat. I hold my hands in my lap to stop them shaking. The water jug is empty and I want to ask the waiter for more, but the sight of the plate he sets in front of me dries up my words.

'Don't wait for us.' Oliver beams at me. 'Eat up while it's hot. That's what my old mum used to say.'

'Everyone's mum says that,' Sylvia empties her wineglass.

I stick my fork in the heap of glistening entrails. A dead fish with staring eyes arrives for Sylvia. It is cosseted with carrots and broccoli and little potatoes in their skins like baby turds. John has a steak. At least it is cooked.

'Gosh, this looks good.' Oliver's white hands flap together like seal fins over a huge plate of mussels. I remember a meal of cockles, sharp with vinegar, slices of bread thickly buttered. Saturday tea-time. The TV on in as we sit at the kitchen table. My father's fist raised to my mother, his body leaning over the table, the muscles of his back straining against the striped ticking of his shirt, his buttocks filling the navy trousers, the thick leather belt defining his waist, his masculinity, silently underlining the threat. My mother pressed herself back in her chair, but her face was defiant.

'Yer silly fat cow.' I remember the disgust in his voice.

'Do you shop at Florival?' Sylvia digs brown flesh away from the spiky bones and shovels it up.

'Sometimes,' I say although I don't know where she means. She is pulling me away from the sharp smell of vinegar and I feel confused. I twirl greasy worms on my fork. My stomach is already full of radish. It pushes out my waistband.

'They've got a super range of casual separates,' Sylvia sounds like a TV ad.

'I'd like some more water,' I say to John and my voice is high, querulous. My mother and father still hover in the shadows. John gives me a 'don't start' look but signals the waiter.

'How's the pasta?' Oliver asks round a mouthful of something slimy.

'I'm not very hungry.' I put my fork down. John gives me a vicious look. We made a bargain before we came out. I wouldn't mention calories and he wouldn't criticise me for not eating enough.

John would like to force me to eat. He's tried all sorts of things to make me do what he wants but I still control my own body.

My mother used to toast crumpets when I came home from school in the winter. They were the best times, before my dad got home from work, when we had the house to ourselves. We'd sit by the fire with a big plate of squashy crumpets running with butter.

. 'If I want to be fat, I'll be fat,' Mum would say, butter loosening her lips. She'd stare angrily at the back door, as if she could see through it, could see him already, coming up the street.

If I want to be thin, I'll be thin. There's nothing John can do about it. John and his boss are getting on well. I won't spoil it for him. I haven't said a word out of place and I've even eaten a whole half radish.

Sylvia is poring over the dessert menu.

'The pudding's the best thing, don't you think?' She tries to drag me into that feminine world of chocolate and indulgence. I smile. She's like a kid in a sweetshop. No sex life I guess. Oliver doesn't look much fun. Neither is John for that matter. He says he likes something to get hold of.

He thinks I don't know about what he gets hold of, but I do. I've seen her mooning at him in the office on the few occasions I have been there. I've heard the change in her manner when she answers the phone to me. She's got a fat arse. John can't help looking when she's not sitting on it. Lately there have been so many excuses, working late at night, day seminars, weekend conferences.

I've kept my promise. I've been very well behaved tonight, very careful, but when we get home, it will be payback time. I've already dissolved the senna tablets in water, so that I can just slip the solution into the coffee pot. I only do it occasionally, so he won't get suspicious. It gives me a lot of satisfaction to hear John blaming whichever restaurant we have eaten at for poisoning him. It justifies my dislike of eating out. It stops John from getting too fat as well.

'Would you like to stop by at our place for coffee?' John asks as we are putting on our coats.

'Great idea.' Oliver slaps John on the back and reaches in his inside pocket for his credit card. Sylvia gives him a look, but says nothing. Her mouth sets in a resigned line as she fusses in her handbag for a tissue.

It won't do them any harm. They could both do with losing a bit of weight. They probably know all about that fat creature in the office so it serves them right anyway.

I feel much better now that we are leaving the restaurant with its torturing smells. I smile as the fresh air hits my face. Tomorrow John won't be going to work and I will be starting a new diet.

Half-Known Things

It rained the day they buried Jamie Q. The whole estate turned out. After all, the kid had only been thirteen, caught in the crossfire. That was the official line, but on the estate people knew different. There was more to it than that.

People knew who had done it. Even Shirley knew. Wasn't her own Haydn knocking round with Flick Johnson, one of the fringe members of the Engineers?

But like Shirley, people only half-knew. It was something you kept in a corner of your mind when you were chatting in the street or hoovering up: something you could banish altogether while Big Brother was on or while you were having a laugh at the pub quiz on a Thursday night.

It was in those sleepless quiet hours when the kids were in bed that the worries came gnawing, about where you were and how safe you were. Shirley had many nights like that, wondering how she was going to make life work for Tonia, who was so light and pretty, so delicately beautiful that Shirley could scarcely believe that she and Pitt had actually produced her. Tonia's dreams were beautiful too, of riding horses, working in stables, even becoming a vet. This was what kept Shirley awake at night, trying to work out how to nurture Tonia as she prepared to blossom on the shit heap that was the estate.

And then there was Haydn, already well known to the police, running round with the Engineers, Flick Johnson knocking on the door. Look what had happened to Jamie Q. In her heart he was still her little boy, but she'd looked at him this morning in the churchyard, before he'd disappeared in the crowd, seen the beard trying to grow on his cheeks, seen the hardness already in his eyes and she'd known she was going to lose him.

Shirley let herself into her house, took off her coat and put the kettle on. It was only when she reached into her handbag that she realised she was out of cigs. She could have done with something stronger than coffee but there was nothing in the house. She'd gone back to the Seven Stars after the funeral but it hadn't been the kind of send off where you sat round eating sandwiches and getting pissed and shooting the shit about what a good life the dead person had lived. Everyone felt bad and didn't know what to say to the family because on the one hand Jamie

146

should have had all his life in front of him but on the other he'd been a nasty piece of work even at thirteen, already heavily involved with the Malt Way mob.

And then Shirley felt herself in a funny position too, knowing how Haydn was getting attached to the Engineers, she herself working behind the bar in the Engine, the gang's home base. She'd only eaten half an egg sandwich at the pub, and that had stuck in her throat.

She'd looked round for Haydn, hoping he'd come back with the crowd, but he'd gone off, probably to Pitt's even though he was supposed to stay with her since his latest exclusion from school because Pitt's smack habit and criminal record meant that he wasn't allowed to have Haydn to stay. That was the court's decision, but Haydn continually flouted it, abetted by Pitt and Shirley got tired of trying to drag him back.

She went into Haydn's room looking for cigs. The mess in there was in sharp contrast to the neatness of the rest of the house. She rummaged through all the shit on top of the chest of drawers, then opened the top drawer. It was as if it jumped out and hit her in the chest. Her breath hitched in her throat, then she laughed. It was a toy. She stretched out her hand. It was real. She could tell by the serious cold feel of it. It was black, dull, squat, like some horrid toad, something totally alien in the homely mess of a young boy's bedroom.

'He's growing up. Going to the bad,' Shirley's mum kept saying, but it wasn't true. He was still just a child. Shirley pulled her hand away. She wanted to pick it up, heft the weight to test its reality, but she was desperately afraid of it. She closed the drawer and backed out of the room, still staring through the wood. She couldn't get the picture of it out of her mind. Her breath was coming in gasps, her chest tightening and squeezing. She crept down the stairs and into the kitchen, felt in her handbag and took two puffs of her inhaler.

Haydn didn't come back all afternoon. Shirley waited for Tonia to come home from school, smoking cig after cig and watching out of the window for the flash of Haydn's purple bike. She'd walked twice round the estate looking in his favourite haunts to no avail. She'd thought she'd caught sight of him and Flick Johnson riding away from the Engine but there was no way she could run after them. Ahmad, the shopkeeper said he'd come in around one o'clock with a couple of the older Engineers.

'He's like the fucking invisible man.' Shirley tried to make a joke but Haydn's badness and her own inability to control him was in the way Ahmad looked at her and in

148

the awkward space across the counter between them. Like everyone else, Ahmad half-knew things. He had to make a living. She walked home slowly, breath catching, hoping Ahmad hadn't been able to see the picture in her mind. It was still so vivid, the drawer opening, her hand reaching in.

Tonia bounced in at three-thirty, still neat after a whole day in her school uniform. She threw her school bag on the kitchen table. 'Can I go to the library, Mum, I've finished my books?' She opened the fridge, poured herself a glass of Coke.

'You seen Haydn?' Shirley's chest tightened with the effort to talk. Her whole body still seemed paralysed by the image of the gun lying amongst Haydn's underpants. She reached for the inhaler.

'No.' Tonia grimaced. 'Didn't he go with you?' She stood still for a moment, even she knew about Jamie Q, but she wasn't old enough to think much about death or to worry about what had happened and whose fault it might be.

'Run off afterwards, didn't he?' Shirley lit another cig.

Tonia sighed. She hadn't much time for Haydn. 'He's a pig, Mum. Never mind.' She threw her arms round

Shirley's neck, then before Shirley could respond she was gone, skipping up the stairs.

What if Tonia went in Haydn's room, opened the drawer? Shirley's mouth went dry but she knew Tonia never went into Haydn's room. When they'd both been small, he'd played with her and she'd followed him everywhere but the last couple of years, since he'd started to change, get in with that bad crowd, he'd ignored her at best and bullied her at worst, so that the poor kid was half-terrified of him now. She wouldn't dare go in his room. But what if she did?

Tonia ran down the stairs just as Shirley heaved out of her seat. Her arms were full of books. 'Please can I go to the library, Mum?'

'I'm working.' Shirley stubbed out her cig. 'You're having tea at your nan's, remember? She might take you after. It's open late tonight. Be a good girl, go up and get washed and changed.'

She waited until she could hear Tonia running the bathroom taps, then she got her address book out of the kitchen drawer and looked for the number. She picked up her mobile and looked at the blank screen. She could see the gun lying in the drawer. Tonia's books sat on the table. They all had pictures of horses on the covers. Shirley lit another cig and called the police.

Take Care What You Ask For

Cardossan Castle, Ayrshire, Scotland 1422.

The crofters of Cardossan trembled in their cottages along the shores of the Black Loch. News had spread quickly that the laird's wife Margaret had given birth to yet another girl child; the ninth in a row, those who could count numbered on their fingers. The very ground shuddered as the laird thundered out of the castle gate, lashing the flanks of his grey mare much as he would have liked to lash his wife.

Inside the birthing chamber Margaret lay sobbing on the blood and sweat-stained bed. The midwife and the women servants went about their business silently, too shocked by the laird's outburst on seeing the child to offer comfort to their mistress. The baby cried lustily as the midwife washed her. A good strong child like all her sisters, the midwife thought, feeling the waving arms and legs, with perhaps her father's temper. The infant howled, red-faced, unaware that she was a source of misfortune for all those in the household and everyone else who came under the laird's jurisdiction.

It was late that night when Donald, the laird of Cardossan returned, his temper much worsened by the drink he'd consumed with his cousins at nearby Drumlore castle. Margaret slept the exhausted sleep of the new mother in the fresh-scented marital bed but that did not stop her husband roughly shaking her awake, pushing his snarling face close to hers as she opened her eyes.

'Yet another puling girl!' he shouted. 'Why has God cursed me with a wife such as you?'

Margaret knew better than to try to protect herself. She lay unresisting in her husband's grip. 'Nine of 'em, all costing a fortune to raise,' he went on, throwing her back on the bed and stamping around the chamber. 'For two pins, I'd cast ye out and find me a proper woman that can breed a son.'

Margaret made no reply, knowing this was an empty threat. There was no way he could raise a legitimate heir by another woman, while yet she, the true wife lived. And while she knew that Donald would not scruple to do away with her if he thought he could get away with it, she also knew that he would not dare raise a hand against her with her father living in the next county.

154

Donald was relying on her family's wealth to finance the repairs that were needed to his castle, having squandered his own family fortune on his hunting, drinking and gambling lifestyle. In fact that was the sole reason for their marriage union as he was fond of telling her. She was under no illusion that the regular couplings which had resulted in their numerous offspring had anything to do with love but were, in Donald's mind, purely for the purpose of providing him with the heir he so deeply desired.

'Useless she-dog,' Donald shouted, punching the walls in order to keep his hands off his wife. There was no prohibition on tongue-lashing though and he treated her to a choice combination of oaths while she waited for him to wear himself out. Her silence however, only served to work him into greater fury and he returned to the bed and gripped her by the throat, dragging her terrified face up to his. 'Of what use are ye to me at all,' he hissed, shaking her all the while, 'Ye're no but a burden, a great millstone, 'twould be better for all if ye were at the bottom of the Black Loch, and mark my words, lady, if the next child should be another useless girl, to the bottom of the Loch ye will go. I promise ye I will see to it myself.'

Margaret's eyes rolled up as she lost consciousness and with an oath, Donald threw her limp body back on the bed and strode off to take his pleasure with his favourite serving-maid.

Three months later

Margaret stared out of the window at the waters of the Black Loch. The eldest six of her daughters ran about on the rocks below, at the water's edge. They were like wild things with their skirts tucked up revealing their strong white legs.

A threatening sky hung over the scene, almost as dark as the black waters it met. Margaret stroked her stomach absently. Pregnant again – her mind was a turmoil of hope and fear. Pregnancies year after year seemed to be all she knew, all she could remember, as if she was a prize cow, yet so far a faulty one – in her husband's eyes.

She'd hoped perhaps there would be no more births; she was approaching the time when the opportunity would come no longer but she knew Donald would never give up on his desire for a son. If she should have proved to be infertile he would seek some way of ridding himself of her. She was in a cleft stick whatever happened for if she produced yet another girl…

Her hands felt her belly again, probing now as if seeking evidence of the child's sex although of course that was impossible. She had often heard the servants chatter of consulting Caitir Colquhoun, the witch who lived in the forest and she'd been tempted to seek a charm herself that might bring about the desired male baby but such was the Devil's business and Margaret felt sure her safety, body and soul, lay in the protection of marriage, the Church and the presence of her wealthy and powerful father.

The laughter of her girls floated up and Margaret smiled despite her worries. The castle was a happy place when Donald was away carousing. She closed the casement and went down to the nursery where Agnes and Mary were eating their dinners. The wetnurse had just finished feeding Anne and Margaret touched a finger to the baby's cheek as she cooed contentedly in her crib.

'She's a fine wee bairn,' said the nurse and Margaret nodded.

'There's soon to be another, Morag,' she whispered.

'Praise be,' said Morag but her eyes were watchful.

'Pray to God it will be a boy,' Margaret said.

Spring spread into summer and all too soon daylight began to fade early as autumn mists swirled up off the loch. Margaret's belly grew heavy and so did her heart. The natural joy she should have felt at the forthcoming birth was doused by her husband's continued ill-temper and threats and by her exhaustion at the thought of yet another childbed. In her heart she felt sure she carried another daughter.

On a dull, damp September day Margaret fidgeted at the window of her chamber. Jennet and Jean, her two eldest daughters played cards quietly by the fire. The other children were confined to the nursery where they could not be a source of annoyance to their father who was entertaining a clutch of drunken friends in the castle's receiving rooms.

A movement outside caught her eye and she spied a horse and rider hastening out of the forest and along the path that skirted the lochside. The horse was black, the rider clad in black with a dark plaid thrown over and their speed confirmed Margaret's instinctive thought that the messenger brought no good news. Her hands shielded her stomach as the child kicked inside her while she watched the stranger ride up to the castle gates.

She received the news of her father's death with a face set in stone. A great wailing went up from her daughters and the castle servants but Margaret saw the satisfied grin on her husband's face and knew she was now at his mercy. Her inheritance of Clairgowr Castle and all its lands would fall to him to squander as he pleased. She let no tear fall until she was safely alone in her own chamber then she cried bitterly until Morag came in with little Anne so that Margaret could spend time with her before she was put to bed. The baby was standing now and trying to toddle and Margaret could not help smiling through her tears as the infant lifted her arms to her mother.

'What will become of us?' she murmured, smothering the baby cheeks with kisses. Morag stood back respectfully. The noise of wild voices, Donald's louder and drunker than all the rest, rose between them.

'God help you now, Ma'am,' Morag ventured.

Margaret nodded, passed the baby back to her. 'Pray for me,' she asked.

Morag hesitated. 'There is another way,' she murmured.

Margaret shook her head and turned away, but later alone in her bed, Morag's words returned to haunt her thoughts.

She should have sent Morag, it was not for a laird's wife to be seen visiting a wise woman but Margaret knew that trust was a fragile thing and if a whisper came to her husband he would not rest until any confidant was broken and spilling her secrets like a shattered pot of peas. She took great care to disguise herself, telling the servants she was grieving and needed to be left in peace. Locking her chamber door, she stole out through the servants' quarters when all were at their supper.

In the gloaming of early evening the forest was dark and ominous with the unseen fluttering of myriad birds seeking their roosts. The wood tried and tricked her with its sly twisting paths, tripped her with tree roots and mossy slips till she felt quite lost but at length she saw a faint glow and smelled the smoke of the witch's fire. She crept up quietly but Caitir Colquhoun's senses were quick and she called out, 'Whisht, show yourself, ye cannae hide from me.'

Margaret came out from the cover of the trees. The witch was not as old as she had supposed, probably in her forties, much like herself.

'I – I need your help,' Margaret stammered. The woman's sharp features and piercing eyes frightened her. Without thinking her hands went to her stomach.

Caitir Colquhoun's eyes followed the movement and she laughed. ''Tis a little late for that, my lady.'

Margaret bit her lip. So her disguise was useless. 'No, you don't understand.' She clutched her belly tightly as if to protect it from the witch's gaze. 'I have nine daughters already.'

'Aye, I know the tale,' Caitir looked her up and down.

'I suppose I'm the talk of the district,' Margaret sighed.

The witch didn't disillusion her but poked at a small bird that was roasting over the fire.

'This next child must be a boy.' Margaret pressed on. 'I thought – a spell?'

''Tis doubtful,' Caitir stared into the fire. 'The child is likely already formed.'

'But it has to be!' Margaret cried in terror. 'My husband has sworn to drown me if there is another daughter.'

The witch looked up and her green eyes flashed. 'I'm a wise woman, not the Good Lord. Only he can work miracles.'

Margaret dissolved into tears.

'There may be something,' Caitir's voice took on a wheedling tone. 'What have you brought in payment?'

'I have no money.' Margaret began.

'And money is little use to me,' the woman replied. 'Let me see.' She held out her hand for the bag Margaret carried. Inside was a lump of butter and one of cheese wrapped in coarse linen, a roasted chicken still warm from the castle kitchen and one of Margaret's own fine wool petticoats. ''Twill do,' Caitir said casually, although her face lit up as she ran her hands through the folds of the petticoat. 'Wait here.'

She went into her hut of branches and skins. Margaret waited and waited, drawing her plaid close round her shoulders as the last warmth of the day departed. The bird over the fire was burning and she drew it away, laying it on a cracked china plate that sat ready, no doubt acquired from another of the witch's clients. At last Caitir emerged with a crude clay cup and a small leather bag.

'Drink this,' she commanded and as she stood over Margaret she seemed to have grown in power and stature.

Margaret hesitated, she could see nothing except a dark muddy surface. 'Do you want to live?' the witch hissed and the brutality of the question shocked Margaret into lifting the cup to her lips. As she swallowed the tangy liquid Caitir reached into the bag and threw a handful of leaves onto the fire. There was no explosion of colours, no visions, as Margaret had half-expected from the servants' tales. The leaves simply curled and crackled as the flames consumed them but for a few seconds there was a dead silence throughout the forest and a sense of all living things watching and listening.

''Tis done,' said the witch, sitting down with a satisfied grunt and reaching for the plate with the charred bird. 'I promise you, whatever comes to you, 'twill not be death by drowning.'

In the depths of January Margaret's labour began, in the middle of the harshest winter she had ever known, bitter as her own thoughts. The snow lay inches deep and for once the Black Loch was white with a crust of solid ice. Margaret watched the villagers sliding and skating on the surface, her own daughters among them. Their joyful shouts rang out across the frozen landscape and up to the castle windows. 'At least I am safe from drowning for the

163

time being,' she thought, turning away as another contraction twisted her body.

'It's a boy,'

The silence in the birth chamber gave way to cries of relief and laughter. Margaret fell back on the bed exhausted, tears cascading down her face.

'The Lord heard our prayers,' Morag said, bathing her mistress's face with a damp cloth.

'Aye,' Margaret agreed, but she knew it was the witch's charm that had worked the magic.

There was great joy throughout the laird's lands when the news was announced, especially as the laird, with uncharacteristic generosity, declared that a great feast would be held to celebrate the birth. The child was christened quickly, as was the custom; his father choosing the names, Allan, Donald, Robert, but his mother was not present at the ceremony. Margaret lay in her darkened chamber, tossing with childbed fever while her attendants could only watch and pray.

The rest of the castle came alive, the laird in high good humour, well wishers calling constantly and the kitchens bustling with preparations for the feast which was to be held outdoors due to the great numbers involved. The land and the loch were still frozen solid and the laird gave orders for huge fires to be lit, to warm the guests and to roast the oxen, deer and whole pigs to feed the multitude. There were tables of salads, syllabubs and custards for the gentry, broth, bread and more importantly, a generous supply of wine and ale for the crofters. It was a rare excitement that would be talked about for many years.

On the day itself, the laird and his cronies were drunk before midday and it was not long before the rest of the company followed his example. They fell on the roasted meats; the dainty dishes and the rough bread all disappeared down hungry throats, accompanied by endless draughts of ale and strong drink.

The light was waning when Donald, drunk beyond sense, shouted, 'My son, where is my son – he should be here, fetch him at once.'

''Tis too cold for a newborn bairn,' one of the ladies dared to remonstrate but Donald was having none of it. He dispatched a servant to fetch the child and after several minutes Morag appeared carrying the infant smothered in a bundle of wool and fur.

'My laird, this is foolhardiness,' Morag kept her eyes down but there was a flash of emerald fire from under her lids. 'Let me take the bairn back inside.'

'Give him here,' the laird shouted, seizing the bundle from her. He lifted the baby aloft to the darkening sky, swinging round in a circle before the assembled crowd, who watched in frozen silence. 'My son, my son,' the drunkard roared to the heavens, 'Praise be to God.'

'Praise God,' everyone mumbled.

'A toast!' the laird, shifted the child to the crook of one arm, seizing his tankard in the other. The company assented but the rattle of drinking vessels was lost in a sudden thunderous clap of sound. All felt a shiver as great cracks appeared in the ice running from the various dying fires, joining up to make an island which circled the whole congregation. They had just time to glimpse the black water beneath before the floe cracked up and all fell into the icy loch.

Their cries were few as they succumbed quickly to the shock of the freezing water. The sounds rose faintly into the air and up to Margaret's window. Disturbed, she turned and muttered before falling back into a peaceful sleep.

Striking Shona

'Striking' he had called her. He'd said it admiringly and looking at herself in the mirror, Shona knew he was right. All her friends said she ought to be a model.

Her skirts, usually leather and usually black were as short as her legs were long. Her hair, short and spiky, was jet black, striking against bright red lipstick and nails. She liked to look different, stand out from the crowd. She painted her last fingernail and thought how the varnish really did look like viscous blood.

'Striking,' she said to herself, savouring the word, a tiny smile playing round her lips. It was true. She drew looks wherever she went, exactly as she intended. She thought how it would be to be famous, pictures in the papers, courted by stars, the playboy rich.

She swivelled before the glass, looking critically at her slim waist and boyish hips. Her figure was perfect but what had attracted Clancy most was her hair. He was funny about her hair…

The doorbell began playing its version of *Strangers in the Night*. Shona grabbed her bag and rushed out of the bedroom and down the stairs. She didn't want any of her family answering the door and seeing Clancy or they would have something to say. They always had something to say.

She needn't have worried. Her mum and her sister Lynda were slumped in front of the telly watching *Coronation Street*. Her dad wasn't in yet, probably stopped off at the Legs of Man on the way home. She made a mental note not to go in there with Clancy. Her dad would have something to say all right about her going round with an older man.

The bell was still ringing, now performing, *Moon River* brightly without feeling. She eased herself seductively round the front door and plopped into Clancy's waiting embrace. She kept an eye out for nosy neighbours, at the same time allowing him a quick feel before pushing him away.

'You'll spoil it,' she complained, shoving his hands away from her carefully contorted hair. In the car, she made herself comfortable. It was nice having a bloke with a car. It was a compensation for his age. She let him ruffle the short edges of hair at the back of her neck.

'Fetishist,' she giggled. 'You're kinky about hair.' He laughed but looked at her nervously. 'I don't mind,' she said, giggling again and he relaxed.

'Where to tonight?'

'I don't mind.'

'McDonalds?'

'You always want to go there.'

'Because it's where we met. It reminds me how lucky I was to find you.'

'That's sweet.' She pouted crimson lips and reached into the glove compartment, riffling through his crummy CDs, looking for something remotely modern.

McDondalds was busy but not crowded, catering to the tea-time trade of late shoppers and early revellers grabbing a bite before a night on the town.

She wolfed the last of her Big Mac and crumpled her empty French fries bag. 'That was good Clance, I was so hungry.'

'There's something I've been wanting to tell you, Sho,' he said as if he'd been waiting for her to finish. She looked up from her chocolate milkshake, a finger of alarm touching her at his serious tone.

What could it be? But he was smiling at her gently. She felt reassured. She really liked the way he smiled and when he looked at her like that she thought maybe she could keep him interested, even though he was so much older than her. She was pretty keen on him really. He was much better than the pimply, punky lads she'd been out with before, with their big mouths, empty pockets and anxious little cocks.

Clancy had class. So what if her girlfriends laughed because he was – what– twelve years older than her, worked in an office and wore a suit? She'd had enough of being groped on park benches, drinking cans of lager for light relief, a joint or two if things got really lively.

Clancy took her out, bought her drinks, meals, little gifts. He had a nice car, even had his own home. Of course he liked to get his hands on her just like all the others but so what? Fair exchange was no robbery. So far it had only been hands. At first she had been flattered, sensing respect in his restraint but lately she had begun to wonder why he still held back. She was ready, starting to get restless even. She kept pushing away vague feelings of irritation, telling herself he was just waiting for the right time, the right place.

'Shona, did you hear me?' He caught her hand across the table. She could feel his knees pressing against hers.

A worried frown crossed her face. She felt uneasy when he looked so serious. She sucked on the straw in her milkshake and waited.

'I… didn't tell you this before. We were…well, we were only just getting to know each other. I didn't know whether it was going to be important.' He stared at her. His eyes were green and his hair was black and shiny, black as her own but his was floppy while hers was teased into stiff spikes.

He touched her face, his fingers sliding into her hair where it lay in points on her cheeks. 'You're lovely you know Sho…'

'What is it?' she cried impatiently, jerking her head away from his hand.

He took a deep breath. 'Shona – before I met you – a long time before, I used to be married.'

She stared at him, mouth hanging open.

'She died,' he said quietly. 'Three years ago. I thought I ought to tell you, that's all.'

'What happened?' Shona whispered.

'Karen was always getting depressed, about nothing really.' He sighed. 'She'd been seeing psychiatrists on and off for years before we met. At first she seemed fine, then she just went down and down. Nothing seemed to help. One day she committed suicide.'

'How?' Shona breathed

'Nothing spectacular,' Clancy muttered. 'She took an overdose of tranquillisers and got in the bath. I found her when I came home from work.'

Shona stared. She didn't know what to say. 'I never thought about you being married,' she said at last. 'Was she pretty?' she asked. Prettier than me? She thought.

'She had the most beautiful hair,' he said. 'It was long and this wonderful deep red-brown colour. It came down almost to her waist.'

He made stroking motions with his hands and she could see he was lost in the memory. A stab of jealousy stung her and she instantly resolved to grow her hair out long and flowing and dye it red – brilliant red. She looked down at the remains of her milkshake, chocolate foam clogging the sides of the waxed cup. A small boy and girl ran round their table, chasing a yellow balloon. The restaurant was filling up, getting noisier.

'When she did it,' she said slowly, 'was it in the same house, where you live now?'

'There didn't seem any point in moving. I'd always liked the house. It's handy for my job and I had happy memories there.'

'I've never seen your house,' Shona said, screwing her straw up and jamming it into her cup before cramming the lid back on. She didn't look at Clancy but stared at the people queuing up for their orders at the other side of the room.

'Would you like to?' he asked softly. He didn't seem to mind her lack of reaction. His hand stroked her knee under the table. 'We could go there now?'

'Okay.' Shona stood up before he could change his mind. She zipped up her leather jacket, swung her bag over her shoulder and took his arm. 'Let's go.' She fluffed her hair with her other hand. Tonight's the night, she thought with a sense of triumph.

The house was small, only a terrace but modern. It was in a nice part of town, a far cry from the run down council estate where Shona lived.

She took in the paved front garden with its central flowerbed. Daffodils speared upwards, stiff buds standing from the foliage. In the dark she couldn't see if they showed yellow promise of flowering.

Neat, she thought, clean and neat. The windows were clean too, with plain curtains, nothing fancy, nothing striking. Inside was the same: bright, clean, plain colours: not overtly masculine but nothing to show a woman had lived here either. Shona was a little disappointed. That was really what she was looking for, clues to the other woman, what she had been like.

That was stupid, she told herself. The wife was long dead, no need to be jealous. Still, her gaze wandered, looking for photographs but there were none. She moved over to the old-fashioned music system, he even had a player for vinyl records. She rummaged through the records and CDs. 'Clance, you really need to get some decent sounds.' She looked up in disgust from a disc of Bruce Springsteen.

Clancy laughed. He had been leaning against the front door, watching her investigation. Now he moved off towards the kitchen.

'Want some coffee?'

'I need to pee,' she said, wanting to see upstairs.

'I'll show you where,' he fell into her trap so easily, leading the way up the open staircase.

'What's in here?' She stopped in front of the first door on the landing.

'Nothing, just a spare room.'

She stretched her hand to the doorknob. He pulled her away, snaked an arm round her waist.

'Come and see my room.' He gave her a squeeze as he opened the second door. It was neat but unremarkable, done in shades of grey.

'Do you always invite girls into your bedroom?' she teased, arching her body against his, inviting him with her lips.

'I've never brought a girl here before. No one's been here since Karen died. There haven't really been many girls. When Karen was alive she was very jealous, jealous of anyone I spent time with. She used to read things into simple friendships. So afterwards, well I'd sort of lost confidence in talking to girls.'

'You weren't backwards at coming on to me that day in McDonalds,' Shona giggled.

'That's because you were so striking, I just had to pluck up my courage. I couldn't believe it when you agreed to a date. I never thought I had a chance.'

'But now you've got me.' She put a foot behind his heel, leaned back, let her weight pull her over, falling back on the bed and clutching him, taking him with her.

'I thought you wanted a pee,' he said, surfacing from a prolonged kiss.

'It can wait,' she whispered, trailing her lips across his cheek, revelling in his hands on her body. She wriggled accommodatingly as he pulled at her clothes then lay in her best black undies, watching as he stripped off his jeans and sweatshirt.

He had a nice body for an old man, she thought. Just the right amount of hair. Just the way she liked it. 'Shall I grow my hair out long?' she asked, fluffing out the black spikes.

'Don't be daft, Sho, I like it just the way it is.'

She thought how soft his eyes were as he admired her, thought she saw love there.

His hands were expert. Another advantage of maturity. He knew all the right places. She was soon hooking her legs up around him, making it easy for him to enter. Her excitement was heightened by the luxury and freedom of doing it in a proper bed with no chance of being disturbed. It was a change from park benches and the back seats of old bangers. Was there a thrill too in making it in someone else's marriage bed? 'Someone dead' a little voice murmured in her mind but she let the waves of sensation drown it out.

Something was wrong, the expected penetration didn't come. She rubbed her body against him, felt his hand between her legs, fumbling now to no avail. She couldn't see his face. His head was pressed below her chin, against her breast. She could feel the sweaty tension of his muscles as he tried too hard. She kissed the top of his head, felt between his legs with greedy fingers. She had a deft hand, despite her youth but nothing worked. He stayed soft and limp.

He rolled away, face hidden in the pillow. 'I'm sorry,' he muttered, 'it's being here, it reminds me…'

'It's okay,' she said, trying not to let her disappointment show.

'I'll make some coffee.' He was away down the stairs without looking at her.

'Milk?' he called from the kitchen while she still lay, pondering his inability to perform. Maybe it wasn't just the room. Maybe he was one of those who just couldn't make it at all. It certainly couldn't be anything to do with her. She'd never had any complaints before.

'Mmm,' she answered, 'and two sugars please.' She stretched lazy limbs in the warmth of the bed. Already her mood was rising. Clance would be okay when they were somewhere else. Maybe even if they just tried again later. She knew she could overcome his fears.

She needed badly to pee now. She got up and padded to the end of the landing where she could see a pale pink bath through an open door. It must be the fatal bath. She stared at it. It was smooth and innocent, spotless and shiny. How could he bring himself to use it? She sat down on the toilet to urinate, not taking her eyes off the bath, picturing him coming home and discovering the dead woman lolling in cold water, her long red hair fanned out round a ghostly face.

She shuddered, dried herself, got up and flushed the loo, glad of the everyday noise. She hesitated on the landing, looking at the other door, the room he didn't want her to see. She wondered what was in there that he was so anxious to conceal. 'Try me' the door seemed to say. She moved towards it.

'You'll catch cold,' said Clancy, coming up the stairs with two mugs and a packet of digestives on a tray. Giggling, she scrambled back into bed. They warmed their bodies on each other. The coffee was hot and strong.

When she woke, the walls were peachy pink. She stared for a moment then realised the walls were moving

178

and so was the pink ruffled bedspread she could see when she turned her head.

She was not in Clancy's grey bedroom. She was not in her own room at home and the room was not moving. It was her, Clancy was on top of her and the force of his rhythm jerked her up and down.

The muscles on his arms stood out as he held himself up away from her with each thrust. She looked down and saw with surprise that she was wearing a nightie dragged up and bunched above her breasts, a pink flowered effort that she wouldn't be seen dead in.

'Hey, Clance,' she giggled uncertainly, 'what's this, dressing up games? Don't think much of my outfit.' Her tongue struggled with the words and she felt vaguely alarmed as she tried and failed to recall how she had got in this room. It must be the room behind that door, Clancy had taken her in there after all, but why couldn't she remember? Perhaps she was dreaming, but this was one dream that was turning into a nightmare.

He didn't answer her. She gazed up at his face and saw tears in his eyes. He thrust harder, pounding at her. She tried to move away but his weight pinned her lower body.

'Come on Clance, you're hurting me.' She tried to push him off but she felt too weak and sleepy still. It was easier to surrender.

Clancy didn't seem to see her. His eyes stared blindly into hers and the tears rolled out and dripped on her face. Now she was really frightened.

'Come on, what's wrong with you?' he hissed. 'You're not a lesbian, are you?'

She shrank from the rage and despair in his voice. She opened her mouth to speak but saw he was not talking to her, wasn't aware of her at all.

'What's wrong? There's someone else, isn't there?' He grunted with effort as he pushed into her. 'But you're mine, you'll always be mine.'

'Get off me!' Shona tried to shove him but he came down on top of her, pinning her completely to the bed. She thrashed her head. The peach walls, the pink bedspread, the flowery nightie cartwheeled before her eyes. It all came together in her head, she was wearing a dead woman's nightdress. The open wardrobe with its row of empty dresses, the perfume bottles confirmed it. This was the marriage bed, not the one in the grey room.

Clancy's rhythm speeded. He was pulling her hair, ripping it from her head, really hurting her. She opened her mouth to scream but her mouth filled with hair.

'I love you, I love you,' Clancy whispered in her ear as she gagged and choked. The words spurted out of him with each thrust, his fists knotted in hair at either side of her skull. He jerked and groaned through his orgasm while she shuddered in disgust. He was having sex with a dead woman. The nightie scratched at her with skeletal fingers.

His weight lifted off her suddenly but she was still too weak to move. What had he put in that coffee she asked herself in sudden terror? His eyes were far away as he lifted her from the bed, crooked one arm round her neck. She willed herself to resist but could only manage a feeble push against his chest, so feeble he didn't even notice it.

She felt something on her head and caught sight of herself in the dressing table mirror, saw his fist tangled in long snakes of red-brown hair, watched those dead locks tumble over her own breasts and felt her scalp writhe.

'I can't let you leave me, Karen,' said Clancy, but she wasn't listening. Even as she realised he was carrying her to the bathroom, her mind was still screaming with the question of where that hair had come from.

The girl bit into her hamburger. Jeez it tasted good. She looked across the table and smiled at the guy. He wasn't that bad looking for an old john. She was too tired and too hungry to be fussy anyhow. He'd promised her a bed for the night and it was more than two weeks since she'd slept indoors. She pushed her dirty blonde hair back from her eyes.

There was a picture on the wall opposite. It was a striking face. The caption read, 'Shona Murdoch – missing from home.' The blonde girl knew her slightly. Shona was always showing off about her looks, always going on about wanting to be famous. Well, she'd got what she wanted; her face had been plastered all over the local papers for the last fortnight.

She took another bite of her burger and turned her attention back to her benefactor.

'You've got beautiful hair,' said the john. She smiled at him. Maybe if she played her cards right, he might even let her get a bath.

He is Perfect

Being undead has advantages. Over a millennium you become an expert in your chosen field. Mine is beauty and, oh, my beauty is flawless, for we undead are obsessed with perfection. What else could we crave in our endless lives? Who else can we love but our beautiful, perfect selves?

My hair is raven; it hangs to my thighs, cut once or twice a century. Amongst others, it defines me. On the street, breasts in front, buttocks behind, hair floating freely, who can resist me?

My clothes must be silky, they fit where they touch. Fabrics with feel, silk, satin or leather to stir senses smoothed and refined by time. My colours are red, the colour of blood and black, colour of death, colour of night.

A vampire needs money to polish her beauty. Our tastes are exquisite, learned over aeons. My trade is an obvious choice, being, so to speak, a creature of the night.

This time is the best; no bulky fabrics or baggy petticoats, voluminous drawers or clumsy boots. Oh the freedom of thigh-high skirts; the sensual pleasure of sheer stockings and spiked stilettos, creamy lipstick swirled on crimson lips. The old manners are gone but there are compensations.

Pulling punters is a cinch. Yes, the men are easy. I slide in their cars, spread my long legs for their benefit, enjoying the slither of the stockings on my thighs. I let them glimpse my underwear, split crotch red and black, and the red open fig of my flesh beneath, sweetly perfumed, the perfection of a timeless life. They can't believe their luck.

In the back seat I let them do anything except mark my flesh, spoil my flawless skin. There is some pleasure in their admiration but little else. It's all the same to me, this human fantasy of orgasm.

I let them do what they like and when they are well and truly away they take my shivers of anticipation for lust. Their pitiful; minds imagine that their pathetic efforts excite me. As they are, so they take me to be. The sexual powers of a vampire are legendary of course. A thousand years of practice makes perfect in this as in all else. The poor things don't know what's hit them.

As their senses climb so my tremors grow for I also am excited, but not by sex. As they grunt their way to climax the time comes to take *my* pleasure. Lost in their feeble sensations, they never see my mouth open wide, they miss the vision of my teeth, immaculate in their whiteness.

I wait to feel their thighs go rigid; that's when the delicious moment comes. I slip my fangs into their necks gently so that they hardly feel a nip as I clutch my legs tightly round their flabby bodies, milking their hot semen as I suck sweetly, softly, just enough to satisfy. Though greedy, the undead are not gluttons but like children we must have what we want. Delayed gratification is not a term we can respect.

I rarely leave a wound large enough to notice. Afterwards, as if waking from a trance, they find a love bite, wonder what happened, remember a good time. Nevertheless, word is out on the street that there is a cutter on the loose. The other girls are up in arms, triumphant that the tables are now turned. For once the punters are the victims.

Time to move on. I never stay in one place long enough to be caught. It's one advantage of a footloose career.

Another city. Dark winter days mean I wake early, slipping on my red dress, shrugging into leather boots, long and sinuous to keep the rain from my perfect legs. The cold means nothing to me but my fur coat is slinky round my shoulders.

Red city lights flare in the black, reflected in the dark mirrors of my eyes. Down the street I stride and though they catcall, those who dare not, kerbcrawl past to cheaper meat.

The car is long and low and black, sleek with money. I slow my step and twitch my coat to show my shape. The door swings open as I bend to look and I stop short.

For a moment the universe wavers, its ancient lines dissolving then returning as I stare. A strange sensation rushes through me. It takes a second to identify twin prongs of interest and desire, last felt some hundreds of years ago.

He is perfect. Black hair sweeps back from ivory skin. I offer him red cushions of my lips as I fit myself into the bucket seat. He sips me lightly and I burn as I have never done before, I am sure, though early memories are dim. Time flickers in and out.

Out on the street, the others stare. It isn't done to kiss a client. They are amazed to see me hanging there with half-closed eyes, my hair cascading back. I am amazed myself and shake my drowsing eyes awake. Every muscle, each nerve fibre screams alert, anticipating joy.

I see them staring, they think he is my pimp. I laugh out loud and settle back to watch his perfect movements as the car pulls out. He is oh so beautiful and as the car moves forward through the darkness I resolve to take him even though I have never taken anyone before.

It is not to spare them that we only suck to slake our hunger and our thirst, nor to spare ourselves from detection and persecution. All nonsense those old wives' tales about contamination by a single bite, one evening's feast. Transformation only comes through death. How could we Old Ones bear to live with all our victims, suffer their ugliness, their stupidity as they begin the journey out of slime across the paths of time, a journey we completed long ago?

But he is perfect. I look and think how few of us there are, us Old Ones. How lonely I have been, for decades now have passed since I last met another of my kind.

The car purrs to a halt and it is time. Another strange sensation: fear of the unknown but the thought of something new doubly excites a palate jaded by the limitless steps of time.

His lips trail mine, searing heat and cold shoot through me, real shivers racking now as my nails tear open and explore his clothes. As I expected, perfection, all perfection underneath. Such sweetness must be mine, it is almost a shame that he must die but I have made my decision – if only he agrees to come.

His hands rove my body. I cannot wait much longer, my jaws ache to spread but he makes no move to enter me. It is almost as if he knows there is no pleasure for me in penetration.

He is smiling as he strokes and stirs me. I can hold out no more and show my teeth, shining dreadful sharp. He smiles at me, inclines his head, the white flesh of his neck is perfect. Deep I sink and drink great saturating gulps, the sucking reflex dredging up from some deep pit inside while red waves sweep us both to fusion. Somewhere we are screaming and time was never like this, then it is over and in warm darkness melting I can see us pipistrelli, silhouetted black against a silver moon.

Walker's Legend

As soon as he saw the severed foot, Marcus Jump knew that Walker was responsible.

He stopped short at the open French windows, looking down at the foot which was somewhat battered and chewed. Rory, his red setter who had been let out earlier for his morning inspection of the grounds, had found it first.

Jump's mind went straight to that day in the hospital. Walker's face had been stamped with fury – hatred even. 'You'll pay for this,' he'd spat, waving his twisted leg almost under Sir Marcus's nose. 'Look at it!'

Unruffled and used to threats of civil action, Jump slid and skated. 'It's not that bad,' he finished up, eyeing the mangled leg critically, 'We'll arrange for a raised shoe.'

'You'll live to regret this,' Walker hissed before limping out of the clinic. Sir Marcus could still see the sheep-faced rows of patients in the waiting area, eyes swivelling fearfully as Walker stumped away amid further imprecations.

Well, theatrical tricks like this wouldn't frighten him. He looked up the curving drive but could see no movement except the waving branches of the bushes.

It was a real foot, he ascertained, peering closely down his nose at it.

'Get away Rory,' he snapped as the setter slunk forward, nose twitching at the smell of meat.

He sighed with annoyance. He could hardly ask Maria, his housekeeper, to come and sweep it up. She would have an hysterical fit and Paolo had already taken the Merc to fill up for the morning trip to his private clinic. Anyway, the less they knew about it the better. He wondered idly where Walker had got it. He couldn't leave it there. Even if he locked Rory indoors, some other animal might make off with the evidence.

After a few seconds irresolution he went into the house, dragging the dog behind him. He searched the unfamiliar broom cupboard for old newspapers and a box. Having secured the object, he went into the dining room to wait for his breakfast and call the police. A twinge of indigestion spoiled his appreciation of his boiled egg.

Among his morning mail, Sir Marcus found a bingo card with the number eleven ringed in red, over which he puzzled for some time before leaving for his consulting rooms.

'Cadaverous tissue, definitely,' said Inspector Trotter, looking expectantly at Jump and licking his moustache.

'From where?' enquired Sir Marcus, closing his filing cabinet and turning to look with distaste at the wet tobacco-stained fronds adorning the inspector's mouth.

'Not so sure,' muttered Trotter, 'no grave-robbing reported.' Rain drummed the windows in the short silence.

.What about the mortuaries?' Jump stared over his rimless glasses before ducking his head to rifle another open filing cabinet.

'We're doing that now.' The inspector shuffled his feet. The smell of his own body steaming in wet clothes was noticeable even to him. 'This man Walker…'

'Here are his case notes.' Jump thrust a fat file into his hands. He wrinkled his nose and stepped back. 'Thought I saw him this afternoon at the hospital, among my other patients in the waiting room. Just for a moment, when I looked again he wasn't there.' He shrugged. 'Do you think I'm just being jumpy?'

Trotter smiled, more at Sir Marcus's lack of awareness than at the pun itself. He weighed the file in his hands, thinking.

'It's always possible. Maybe I'd better give you a shadow. Chopping off someone's foot, even if they are already dead, indicates somebody quite determined, if deranged. He's a frequent patient on the psychiatric ward, I'm told – at least since being discharged from your care.'

'Well he doesn't frighten me,' said Jump. 'Just get on with catching him, Inspector. You've got my description?'

'It's a bit vague,' said Trotter, flicking through the file. 'I can't believe a man can be a patient in two separate hospital departments without either producing a picture or a sensible description.'

'I'm sure you'll get one elsewhere,' Jump picked a file out of the cart in front of him. 'These are the days of Big Brother, aren't they?'

'I suppose the deformed leg will help,' Trotter brightened. 'It's a pretty obvious identification.'

A nurse swished through the flowery curtains at one end of the room. 'Mrs Chivers is still upset, Mr Jump,' she murmured.

'Women!' Sir Marcus raised his eyebrows and looked at Trotter for support. 'You'd think a shortened leg was the end of the world. Tell her she can have as many pairs of raised shoes as she can afford, they're not that expensive. I can't spend any more time with her, I've wasted enough already.' He looked pointedly at Trotter and began to move away towards the curtains.

'I'll send a man round,' Trotter called, making no attempt to leave. The rear view of the nurse was attractive, the way the crisp cotton uniform cased her body caused tremors in his underwear. He sat down to scan Patrick Walker's notes but it was all medical stuff of little interest and less legibility, yielding nothing of value except a catalogue of the suffering Walker had endured under Mr Jump's knife.

As he got up to leave, Sir Marcus's voice carried clearly into the office from behind the curtains. 'Yes, I've already explained this Mrs Owens. You will be on crutches for the rest of your life but at least you will be able to get about. There are many people much worse off than you.'

Trotter sighed and gave mental thanks for his health and strength.

193

Sir Marcus climbed out of the Mercedes and watched as the car slid away in the direction of the Chinese quarter of the city where Paolo would get his evening meal. Pushing away faint pangs of hunger he turned to the door of his consulting rooms. A parcel lay on the top step. Rain pattered on its black plastic wrapping.

Even in the dim light of the evening street, the package's dimensions made certain suggestions to Sir Marcus, ideas of such horrid fascination that he neglected to look along the street or even to think how the parcel might have got there. He picked it up, felt its weight and texture, suspicions strengthening as the incoming data backed up his first premise.

Remembering the key in his hand, he hastily opened the door, clutching the heavy package under his other arm. He took it straight to the treatment room where he laid it on the stainless steel trolley and tore at the wrappings without even taking off his overcoat. A small voice in his head reminded him that the package ought to be left unopened for the police but horror and curiosity overwhelmed it.

A gasp of satisfaction escaped his lips as he stood back and looked at the discoloured flesh of the leg, dully contrasting with the shiny black bin liner wrapping. Not surgically dissected but dismembered after death, he decided, analysing the mashed injuries at either end of the footless limb. Coarse, black hair sprouted thickly below, thinly above, the knee. A male leg, muscular, thought Sir Marcus, although you couldn't always tell.

A noise made him look up, suddenly realising his vulnerability. Had he closed the front door? He hurried to check, listening again in the dark, narrow hall. The garden tree tapping at the window, he reassured himself, glancing through the open kitchenette door at the dark square of glass. The fluorescent light in the treatment room buzzed and blazed coldly on the leg and the clean, shiny trolley. All seemed still.

Jump went into the study and closed the door. Here the light was yellow, long shadows softening the antique furniture. He picked up the phone and punched in a number.

'Inspector Trotter's off duty, Sir.' The desk sergeant's voice was thick and slow. 'I'll put you through to CID.'

'We've already sent a man round to your house.' Trotter's replacement said in clipped tones. No tobacco stains there, thought Sir Marcus, picturing a martinet in a Burberry mac.

'But I'm not there,' he protested. 'I had to call at my office for some notes. I'm preparing for a conference at the weekend. And there's a leg here. It was on the step when I arrived.'

There was silence, eventually broken by the faint clicking of a keyboard as the detective scrolled through Trotter's notes.

'It was in a plastic bin liner,' said Sir Marcus in the hope of provoking a response.

'You opened it?' The question was accusing.

'I didn't know it was a leg, did I?' Jump snapped covering his awareness of telling a small lie with irritation. 'There's no foot on it', he said to distract the officer further. 'It probably matches the foot I found this morning.'

'Where are you now Sir?' The voice was patient. Jump rattled out the address. Reminded of his predicament, he peered about the shadows but saw nothing untoward.

'I'll get a man over as soon as I can. Don't touch anything and don't answer the door till we get there. This man is obviously dangerous.'

Sir Marcus felt a quiver of apprehension. 'What if he's already here?' he whispered, remembering the noise at the window.

'Keep him talking and don't antagonise him,' the policeman instructed. 'Now go and check your locks, we'll be there soon.'

Jump put down the phone and listened. The air felt ominous. The furniture seemed to wait. He shook himself, went into the front consulting room and fetched a bottle from the glass cupboard by the faint illumination from the streetlamp outside.. He poured and drank a large brandy before switching on the light.

Walker was standing behind the door, wet hair plastered to his skull. He was holding a large hatchet. He looked very much like a character from a horror film thought Sir Marcus. Observing the dancing frenzy in the man's eyes, he abandoned any hope of reasoning with him.

As Jump made a dive for the door something very heavy hit him on the head and he awoke to find himself roughly lashed face down on the consulting room couch, his arms extended above his head. Some interior research informed him that his hands were tied tightly together at the wrists and his fingers were taped firmly to the head of the couch.

Copper flavoured his mouth and he felt the sticky trickle of blood meander down his cheek and rim the left side of his upper lip. He could not see Walker but he could smell him close and guessed he was standing to one side behind his head.

'Where did you get the leg?' he asked, playing for time. His mouth slurred the words, lips numb. Cymbals crashed in his head. Where the hell were the police?

'It's my brother's,' said Walker as if that explained everything. 'He was a bastard too.'

Jump's eyes caught the shine of the hatchet blade as Walker swung it experimentally. He tried to look up but the bonds held him firmly. He could see part of Walker's legs, cased in dirty black trousers, a bit of an anorak.

Be soon, he prayed mentally, willing the police, anyone, to hurry. Maybe his secretary, Miss Treadwell would return unexpectedly for some forgotten item.

'I'm not going to kill you,' Walker said. He sounded almost sane.

Jump flinched, feeling fingers touch his legs, soft and strangely sensitive. Walker stroked up and down his thighs. Jump felt him trace the outline of his calves, line the major muscles.

He tensed in fear and Walker snickered, letting his hands play on. One hand moved away. Jump felt the movement, saw the hatchet raised in his mind's eye; saw himself in golden sunshine, playing tennis, swimming, running with Rory, strong legs pumping.

'No,' he whispered, tears squeezing out to mingle with congealed blood.

'No,' agreed Walker, 'not your precious legs, Doctor. I want to make sure you don't butcher anyone else – ever again.'

Sir Marcus's screams dissolved in the wail of approaching police sirens as Walker brought down the hatchet on his long, delicate fingers.

Lightning Source UK Ltd.
Milton Keynes UK
UKOW01f0236190716

278655UK00001BA/2/P